STAGECOACH TO HELL

The stage lurched as Coe was straightening out of a switchback. He felt an instant and paralyzing flash of alarm. My God, Coe thought. My nerves are strung tight. The alarm vanished as the stage continued moving, scraping the hewed-out bank and hanging over the steep drop. His mouth opened wide with an un-screamed cry of fear. His tongue was plastered to the roof of his mouth, and he couldn't make a sound. It seemed as though the right rear wheel of the stage just dropped away from the vehicle. Oh Jesus, he thought. I drove off the edge. We're going over.

STAGECOACH TO HELL

by

Giles A. Lutz

The Golden West Large Print Books
Long Preston, North Yorkshire,
BD23 4ND, England.

Brit~~ish Library Cataloguing in Publication Data.~~

Lutz ~~Giles A.~~
~~Stagecoach to ...~~

~~A catalogue record ... this book is~~
~~available from the British Library~~

ISBN   978-1-84262-961-1 pbk

Published in Large Print 2014 by arrangement with
Golden West Literary Agency

The Golden West Large Print is an imprint of Library Magna
Books Ltd.

Printed and bound in Great Britain by
T.J. (International) Ltd., Cornwall, PL28 8RW

CHAPTER ONE

The din in Charley Brown's Congress Hall Saloon was growing steadily louder. But then it always did, at this hour of the night. The liquor flowed freely, and bursts of laughter broke out all over the big room. Nobody talked in a normal voice. If a man wanted to be heard, he tried to outyell all the others.

Coe Dahmer was having a wonderful time. He sat at a table with congenial friends, and his pockets were stuffed with money. Life was his horse, and he was riding it high, wide, and fancy. He remembered his father telling him all a man could expect of life was a little good whiskey to drink and a pair of loose boots.

Coe threw back his head and laughed uproariously at the memory. Hell, he was far beyond the limits Jake Dahmer had set for a successful life.

Coe laughed easily tonight, and the remark didn't have to be particularly amusing to arouse his mirth. Somebody could say something about the weather, and Coe would think it hilariously funny.

He squinted at the men across the table from him and shook his head. Maybe he should start slowing down his drinking. His vision was getting foggy, and he saw a double outline where only one existed before.

He didn't give that inclination enough time to root solidly in his head. He could always handle his liquor, and he didn't see any weakening in that capacity now. This was his night to howl. Maybe he would have to pay for it in the morning, but it had happened before, and he had lived through the misery that came after a night like this. He wouldn't start worrying about something that wasn't even here.

Tonight, he was king of the world. He had six good friends at the table with him. He supposed he could be accused of buying their friendship, for he paid for every bottle that came to the table. The thought didn't worry him. Tonight, he was a thoroughly happy man, and nothing was going to put a damper on his enjoyment.

His happiness showed in his beaming face, in the flash of good, strong teeth, showing every time he threw back his head and laughed. He was a strapping big man, his frame built on a massive bone structure. He was twenty-five years old and that shock of red hair was tousled, the eyes a startling shade of blue. His chin was granite, but it wasn't pugnacious. His hands were huge, with blunt, stubby fingers. Those fingers had a surprising amount of skill. Many men said he could get out more of a six-team span than anybody else in the territory. Coe never completely agreed with that. He would just grin and say, 'Maybe you're right.'

Oh, tonight was his all right. Earlier in the evening, he had sat in on a poker game and had taken almost a hundred dollars out of it. Now he was spending that money and enjoying treating his friends.

Coe picked up the bottle from the table and emptied it. The few remaining drops didn't cover the bottom of his glass. He held up the bottle and squinted down its neck.

'It was almost full not ten minutes ago,' he said plaintively. 'Now look at it. Dry as a bone. I know damned well we didn't drink it.' He stared inquiringly from face to face. 'Did we?'

Grinning faces all around the table answered him with shaking heads. Coe was getting pretty loaded. When he reached this stage, he always came up with something funny.

'I know what's been happening,' Coe said solemnly. 'Ole Charley Brown is a tricky one. He's serving bottles with holes in the bottom. The whiskey runs out through the holes faster than we can drink it. He sells more whiskey that way.' He upended the bottle and stared owl-eyed at its bottom. 'See,' he said triumphantly. 'Big hole right there.'

Men pounded each other on the back, roaring appreciatively at Coe's solution. Coe was a card.

'People ain't got any right to call us a bunch of drunks,' Coe said indignantly. 'Not when we ain't drinking all that whiskey. Gonna have to complain to Charley about his bottles.'

That evoked a new outburst of hilarity. Only one face at the table wasn't joining in the merrymaking. Bill Crawford sat beside Coe, a small, scrawny man with a sour face. He was a dozen years older than Coe. His face was long and thin with a lugubrious droop to the mouth. Crawford rarely smiled, but then, he didn't have a lot to smile about. That crippled leg gave him a lot of pain. His leg had been broken in a bad fall from a horse, and it had never mended properly.

'Hell, Coe,' he said in disgust, 'you're drunk again.'

Coe threw an affectionate arm across Crawford's shoulders. They made an odd pair with nothing in common, but a bond was there. Tucson had grown accustomed to seeing the two together. People might shake their heads at the association, seeing no reason for it. Crawford was a sour, tense man, Coe a happy-go-lucky person without a worry about the morrow. They were no more alike than day and night, yet they seemingly belonged together.

'Ole voice of conscience,' Coe announced. 'Pleased with nothing I do. Always chewing on my ass.'

Hy Simmonds sat across the table. 'I don't know how you stand it, Coe.'

Coe stared slyly around the table. 'I don't want Bill to hear this. But every time he opens his mouth, I got him beat. He doesn't know I'm deaf.'

All around the table, men howled and pounded on each other. It must have been the ridiculousness of the statement that appealed to them. Men swore Coe Dahmer could hear a fly walking across the ceiling.

Either Coe's words or the general hilarity stung Crawford, for he shoved his chair back and stood. Twin spots of color burned in his sallow cheeks. He had taken only one drink, and it wasn't enough to fortify him against the remarks of a bunch of drunks.

Crawford glared at the grinning faces around the table. 'You damned bunch of clowns kill me,' he said fiercely.

'That might not be a bad idea,' Simmons said.

The remark really prodded Crawford's anger. Coe had the taste of a hog when it came to picking his friends. All Coe wanted was companionship. If they furnished that and roared at his sallies, Coe thought he was doing just fine. The poor, damn fool couldn't see the vultures for what they were. They would leave him in a hurry after they picked his pockets clean.

'One thing all of you won't have to worry about,' Crawford shouted. 'You don't have to worry about drinking yourselves stupid. You were that before you started.'

That wiped the mocking grins off of their faces. Three of them scowled, and Hy Simmons jumped to his feet. 'Who in the hell do you think you are?' he demanded wrathfully. 'I'll show you, you can't talk to me like that.'

'Sit down,' Coe roared. He locked eyes with Simmons. Simmons looked away first. Coe Dahmer was a forceful man. It was hard to arouse his temper, but he was awesome when it happened. Coe had torn up Sullivan's saloon a few weeks ago when a couple of strangers didn't realize who they were baiting.

'Damn it, Coe,' Simmons said petulantly as he sat down. 'He ain't got any right to talk to any of us that way.'

Coe grinned. 'Hell, Bill doesn't mean any real harm.' His grin expanded, and his eyes twinkled. 'You know why he rubs people so much? Because he's usually right.'

His booming laugh rang out again. It was infectious enough to put some grudging grins on the faces around him. Nobody wanted to offend Coe. It wasn't smart to offend the man who was buying the evening's liquor.

'Come on, Bill,' Coe coaxed. 'Sit back down. If you don't, you'll miss out on a fun night.'

Crawford was thoroughly worked up. 'Your idea of fun, not mine,' Crawford snapped. 'I've sat around and listened to a bunch of drunks long enough. You go ahead and drink yourself blind. But don't expect me to put you to bed.'

Coe's face burned. 'Don't give me that,' he roared. 'You name me one time when you had to put me to bed.'

'Maybe not,' Crawford conceded. 'But if you keep on the way you're going, it's coming as sure as hell.'

He turned and limped toward the door, his narrow shoulders held stiffly.

The uneasy silence held until Coe broke it by saying, 'Bill doesn't mean anything. The leg gets to hurting him, and he can't stop the words from pouring out.'

'By God, he better learn to hold those words,' Simmons said belligerently. 'At least, around me.'

Coe's eyes turned a different shade of blue, an icy shade. 'You got something in mind, Hy?'

Simmons couldn't meet the impact of those eyes. He popped his knuckles and watched the operation with absorbed interest.

'Aw, Coe,' he muttered, 'I didn't meant it like that.'

'Sure,' Coe said in quick forgiveness. 'Hey, are we going to let a little temper ruin our evening? I say we need another bottle.'

That restored the brightness to their faces. 'You're right, Coe,' a couple of them said in unison. 'You always come up with the right answer.'

Coe caught Flora's eyes. He beckoned to

her and held up the empty bottle.

Flora was one of Charley Brown's girls, and she worked the floor. Years of experience had quickened her eyes. Her earnings depended upon that alertness. Coe was one of her favorite customers. He bought with a free and open hand, and he was always generous.

Flora hurried to the bar, picked up a bottle, and hastened back to Coe's table, a hungry gleam in her eyes. If this was like Coe's other orders, she would be richly rewarded.

Flora was a voluptuous blonde, the ardors of her occupation beginning to show in the tiny lines radiating from the corners of her eyes. The roots of her hair were black. She needed another application of peroxide. In repose, her mouth had a sulky droop, but now a smile was lifting the corners of her mouth.

She set the bottle before Coe. 'Is this what you wanted, Coe?'

'You know it isn't, Flora. But I'll have to settle for another time when everybody isn't watching.'

'Oh, you're awful,' she said coyly. The hungry gleam didn't leave her eyes as she watched Coe fold the bill in his fingers. She couldn't see the denomination on the corner of the bill, but if she knew Coe, it would much more than pay for the bottle.

She leaned toward him, her breathing quickening. Coe liked to tuck the bill into the low-cut bodice of her dress.

Coe plunged his hand deep into the bodice, and his eyes grew round with mock awe. 'You'd never guess what I found down here.'

Flora giggled as she slapped at his hand. 'You stop that, Coe Dahmer.' She blushed, but she wasn't really embarrassed. 'What will people think, watching you do things like that?'

'What do you think, Flora?' Coe drawled. 'That's more important.'

She caressed his cheek with the back of her fingers. 'I'll have to think about that. You ask me later.'

'Maybe I'll do just that,' Coe said. But he had no real interest in her. All of his attention was on getting the cork out of the bottle.

Flora stared at him a long moment before she moved away. The sulky droop had returned to her mouth. Who in the hell needed him?

Coe grinned at the ribald remarks flung at him from around the table.

'You showed a lot of early foot there, Coe,' Simmons remarked. 'But then, you faded out fast. What's the matter? Didn't you find enough to whet your appetite?'

Coe grinned. 'All I wanted to do was to put a little excitement in her life.' He had the cork out now, and he poured himself a generous drink. He raised his glass, trying to think of a toast. His thoughts were getting fuzzy, and all he could think of was something his father told him.

'To loose boots,' he said solemnly.

At some of the blank stares, he roared, 'Would you rather drink to tight boots?'

The blank stares disappeared, and men laughed in appreciation. Coe was in fine fettle tonight.

Coe emptied his glass and waited for the bottle to make the rounds of the table. He looked disapprovingly at the level in the bottle when it returned to him. Damned if he wasn't out with a bunch of thirsty hogs tonight.

He poured himself another drink. Something Crawford said hammered in his mind. Crawford was dead wrong. He wasn't going to put Coe to bed tonight. Coe couldn't remember a single time when he hadn't been able to walk out of a place under his own power. This night wasn't going to be any different.

He ran the glass over and threw back his head and laughed. Everything amused him tonight.

As he raised the glass to his lips, a hand caught his wrist, spilling a good third of the drink.

'Now, that wasn't funny, wasting good whiskey that way. Coe slewed around in his chair and stared up at Jett Kincald's angry face.

'If this is your idea of a joke, Jett, it's in damned poor taste,' Coe said plaintively.

'You're drunk again,' Kincaid said furiously. 'Haven't you got a run in the morning?'

Coe put a firm hand on his rising temper. He always felt this way when he was around Kincaid, and whiskey wasn't responsible for the feeling. He disliked Kincaid, even when he hadn't touched a drop. 'You know I have, Jett,' Coe said reasonably. 'I'm taking the stage to Prescott.'

'Look at you,' Kincaid snapped. 'You're in no shape to drive anyplace.'

Kincaid was a big man, though he lacked Coe's height. His jowls were thickening, and the flab around his belly was growing. Why shouldn't it? Kincaid avoided physical work as though it was the plague. By the paleness of his complexion he looked as though he even avoided the sun whenever he could. He was always tossing his head to keep the great mass of black hair from falling down into his eyes. His eyes were black and unblinking. Their cold steadiness reminded Coe of a snake's eyes. Coe supposed that women found Kincaid handsome, though those cold eyes should have repelled them. Myra, he thought mournfully, what did you ever see in him to marry him?

Kincaid's remark surprised and irritated Coe, and he mulled over the words. 'Jett, that's uncalled for. Did you ever see me when I wasn't in shape to drive?'

Kincaid was working himself into a fine fit of temper, for a wave of red was rising from his collar.

'Don't talk back to me,' he yelled. His fingers bit into Coe's shoulder. 'Get on your feet, and get out of here. That's an order.'

Coe's face darkened. Kincaid didn't need much of an excuse to throw his weight around. Coe jerked his shoulder, throwing off the hand. Nobody manhandled him. He stood, towering a good four inches over Kincaid. His earlier good humor still remained, for he said pleasantly, 'Why don't you have a drink, Jett? Maybe it'll simmer you down.'

Kincaid was speechless for a moment at Coe's daring to talk to him like this.

Coe found it interesting to see the blaze fill Kincaid's eyes. That put a little life in them.

'You drunken bum,' Kincaid shouted. 'I'll teach you some respect. You're fired.'

Coe grinned mockingly. Kincaid had the title, but he didn't have the authority to carry out such a threat.

'Why, boss,' Coe paused, making a deliberate insult of the title, 'you haven't got the say-so. Only Myra can fire me.'

Kincaid's face went tight and pinched, and his eyes were wild. The suck of his breathing was harsh and audible. All the color left his face, leaving it bloodless. Everybody within hearing distance caught Coe's insult. Myra Kincaid's money was behind the stage line. She made the final decisions in everything, and everyone in Tucson knew it.

'Why, goddamn you,' Kincaid said. 'I'll shut your damned mouth for you.' He made a serious mistake. He swung at Coe.

Coe saw the blow coming in time to jerk his head to one side. Kincaid's knuckles scraped his cheek.

Coe was mad enough to ignore the sting in his face. 'You never do get any smarter, do you?' Coe said as he hit Kincaid. It was a good, solid blow, but it went in high, landing on Kincaid's cheekbone, instead of on the chin. It knocked Kincaid backward in reeling, staggering steps, and his arms flailed to regain his balance. The people at the table behind him, scattered to give him room. Kincaid fell on the table, the wood creaking and groaning under his weight. Its legs suddenly collapsed, and the table top split, dumping Kincaid to the floor. He fell heavily, and the two halves of the table fell in on him.

Kincaid struggled to throw the pieces of the table from him. His eyes were pain-glazed, and he stared, unseeingly, up at Coe. The red blotch on his cheek grew. Coe thought it was an improvement. It put some color in Kincaid's face.

The pain must have reached through his muddled senses, for Kincaid raised a hand and rubbed his cheek. The hurt, or the motion, cleared his eyes. Coe had never seen so much venom in a man's eyes. The rattlesnake's coming out in him, he thought.

Kincaid raised his head, but he wasn't foolish enough to try to get to his feet, not with that big figure standing over him.

'You're fired,' he yelled. He was so furious that he sprayed saliva before him. 'Do you hear me? You're fired.' He screamed the last two words over and over.

Coe reflectively rubbed his knuckles. He guessed he had drunk more than he realized. The whiskey had ruined his aim. He should have knocked Kincaid unconscious. He winced at the thought of Myra's reactions when she heard about this. Maybe she would strip off his hide for hitting her husband. But damn it, Kincaid had swung the first blow.

'You're thickheaded, aren't you, Jett?' he said. 'Didn't you hear what I told you? Only Myra can do that.'

Men rushed from all over the room, forming a thick ring of interested watchers around Coe and Kincaid. They were all behind Coe, for he heard several suggestions of what he should do to Kincaid. Kincaid's arrogance didn't make him a popular man around town.

Charley Brown waddled up, pushing his way through the onlookers. He was a portly man, and his belly bounced with each step. Charley Brown was unhappy; it showed in his face.

'Coe,' he said indignantly, 'you know I don't allow rough-housing in here.'

'Hell, Charley,' Coe said plaintively. 'I was

22

just sitting here, enjoying myself, when Kincaid busted in here on the prod. Didn't you see what happened? Jett begged for what he got.'

Kincaid still lay on the floor, but at least he had momentarily quit screaming. 'He forced me, Charley. If you heard what he said to me–' He flushed and bit off the rest of his words.

Coe grinned. 'Go ahead, Jett. Tell Charley what I said to you.'

Kincaid looked balefully at him. 'This isn't done yet, Coe. I promise you that.'

'Oh, shut up,' Brown said wearily. 'This stops right here. Both of you know I don't allow any brawls in here.' His eyes were a little apprehensive. Coe seemed peaceful enough now, but Brown didn't know how long that would last. He sure didn't want Coe breaking loose and wrecking his place as he had Sullivan's saloon.

Brown's jaw hardened. 'I want both of you out of here. Right now! If you're gonna argue some more, you can do it outside.'

Coe sighed. 'If that's the way you see it, Charley. Something always comes along and ruins a good evening, don't it?'

He pulled a few bills from his pocket. That had been a pretty good-sized roll when he first sat down here. Where did all that money go?

He straightened out the bills, peeled one off, and handed it to Brown. 'See that the boys get another bottle, Charley. No sense in ruining their evening too, is there?'

Brown's stern expression softened. He hated to throw Coe out, but he had learned from bitter experience the way to stop a brawl was to step in hard and fast at its outbreak.

He looked at the bill in his hand. 'You've got some change coming out of this, Coe.'

'Give it to Flora,' Coe said. 'Ain't no sense ruining her evening, is there?'

He looked down at Kincaid. 'You want to walk out with me, Jett?' That purplish hue was beginning to steal into Kincaid's face again. Kincaid looked so choked up that he was unable to speak. Maybe it was just as well he didn't. Coe was quite sure he didn't want to hear any part of it.

Coe looked back from the door. Kincaid was just getting to his feet. Nobody had offered him a helping hand. Coe didn't know of anybody who cared much for Kincaid. That gave Coe a poor, sorrowful consolation. It didn't nearly begin to replace all the fun Coe was losing.

CHAPTER TWO

Coe knew every foot of Tucson's streets, every yard of the surrounding roads and highways. He should; if he hadn't walked over those streets and roads, he had driven over them.

Did he love Tucson? The thought had never occurred to him, one way or the other. He had been raised here, and he just naturally accepted it as being his home. He knew one thing for sure. Tucson could be rough weatherwise – hot as hell in the summertime, relatively pleasant in the winter, though Coe had seen too many winter days cold enough to put a frozen cramp in a man's hand. He guessed there was no place in the world where one could be completely happy with the weather the year around.

Tucson was an old town, its history going back to before the coming of the Spaniard. Most of its population was still made up of people of Spanish or Mexican descent. The coming of the Americans had literally kicked Tucson's ass out of its lethargy. Coe

25

had seen most of its growth from a somnolent town into a bustling one, bursting its seams.

Tucson had once been a walled town, but its growth had spilled out of that original protection. The walled portion was called the old presidio. Now the fine, powdery dust of the streets of the old and new sections alike was constantly stirred by the traffic that moved day and night. The old-timers complained bitterly of the changes. The newcomers took advantage of the opportunities the growth afford.

In his few moments of sober reflection Coe could see all the opportunities he had missed. He never let those moments bother him for long. He guessed he didn't have any great desire to climb higher than he was. He was content with his job, and it paid him enough to furnish any need he felt. Crawford had harangued him about his lack of ambition, and Coe accepted it all with a shrug. Why worry about the years ahead? A man had no guarantee that he would reach those years. Coe took each day as it came and thoroughly enjoyed them. He couldn't see where any driving ambition had done Crawford much good. Of course, Crawford had his own business, and he owned his own house. Good for him, Coe thought, and there was no malice or envy in him. All he could see that ambition had done for Crawford was to turn him into a sour, unhappy man.

That's not fair, Coe rebuked himself. Crawford knew pain much of the time from that crippled leg. He grinned as he thought, Maybe Bill is right when he says you should be looking ahead. Maybe you won't even have a job after tonight. He shrugged the unhappy reflection away. He wouldn't believe that anything Kincaid could say would influence Myra against him; not after all the years he had worked for her and her father.

Coe's boot caught on a small stone in the street, and he stumbled. Damn but he must be drunker than he thought, to be shuffling along like this. How Crawford's eyebrows would rise if Coe stumbled into the house like this. Coe chuckled softly. He was still moving along under his own power, and nothing was going to destroy his memory of a thoroughly enjoyable evening.

Coe's face sobered. It had been enjoyable until Jett Kincaid came in. Damn him, Coe thought dispassionately. Kincaid was the kind of a man who ruined everything he

27

touched. For the life of him, Coe couldn't see how Myra stood him. He wished Brad Bannock hadn't died. Brad wouldn't have let his daughter marry someone like Jett Kincaid.

Coe still mourned Bannock's death, though that had been three years ago. He had more than expected to see Bannock's Stage Line fall apart after Brad was gone, but he had underestimated Myra's capabilities. She had stepped in and run things, expanding the line until it was bigger than when Bannock was at the head.

Myra, you did real well, Coe thought sorrowfully, until you married Kincaid. His prediction that the business would go to pieces under Kincaid hadn't come true, either. Myra had a smart head on her shoulders. She might love Kincaid, but she was still aware of his weaknesses. She still made all the important decisions, letting Kincaid strut around with an empty title. Coe snorted. Jett Kincaid couldn't manage anything.

'Brad, I hope you know you raised quite a gal,' Coe muttered. 'It's too bad she couldn't have married somebody worthwhile.'

His thoughts went back to the days he had first gone to work for the Bannock Stage

Line nine years ago. The new line was struggling in those days, threatening to go under at any moment. The last of the Apache outbreaks was just ending, and when a stage went out on a run, it was touch and go that it would return. The loss of another stage would have ended Bannock. Coe had gone to work for Bannock when he was sixteen, doing menial tasks. He had cleaned out more than his share of stalls, and, God knew, he would be a rich man if he had a ten-dollar bill for every team he had hitched to a stage. Nobody could ever accuse him of being lazy, and he had worked up to substitute driver. He had never wanted harm to come to any of the drivers, but he wistfully watched them drive away on each run. They were tough and sturdy men, and nothing ever seemed to happen to them. Often he had doubted he would be here long enough to be a driver. Bannock's money was running out fast. The threat of the Apaches made business poor, and Bannock had to scrounge to pay his help. Coe had watched the taut lines deepen in Bannock's face. Every morning, when Coe reported for work, he half-expected to see the doors locked.

How well he recalled the day that endeared him to Bannock and Myra forever.

29

'I've got two passengers booked for today,' Bannock announced. 'Feel like going along?'

'Hell yes,' Coe replied cheerfully. Bannock couldn't meet expenses with a partial load like this, but he had to keep on going.

Bannock climbed up and took the reins. At Coe's look of surprise, Bannock said, 'Just you and me. We're all that's left.'

'That's all we need,' Coe replied and grinned.

Eight Apache renegades jumped the stage a few miles out of Tucson. Coe didn't know they were anywhere around until he heard their screeching.

Bannock threw a fear-filled look behind him. 'Goddamn those red devils,' he raved.

'Just keep it rolling,' Coe said and slithered out of his seat. He took his rifle with him and crawled onto the stage top. He spraddled out and squinted down the rifle barrel, letting those devils get closer and closer before he fired. The Apaches were close enough for him to see the paint smeared on their faces before he opened fire. The Apaches fired steadily, and some of those bullets passed close enough to Coe for him to hear the humming of the slugs. Bannock screamed at the top of his lungs, though Coe couldn't make out the words. He imagined Bannock was wondering why he wasn't shooting.

A bouncing stage made a poor platform for good shooting, and Coe waited until he could make every shot count. He rode with the lurches of the stage and squeezed off the first shot. The grunt of pleasure was deep in his throat as the nearest Apache threw up his hands and toppled off his pony.

That didn't slow the others. Coe dumped another one and thought that might have made them falter slightly. He fired a third time, and his score was perfect: three shots and three dead bucks in the road.

The others pulled up, howling their frustration. Several of them let go a shot in a final display of defiance.

It must have been one of those shots that got Bannock. Coe heard him gasp, 'I'm hit, Coe. Bad.'

Bannock slumped in his seat, and Coe was afraid he was going to fall into the road.

'Hang on, Brad,' he begged. 'I'm coming.'

Coe scrambled back to his seat, barely reaching it in time to grasp the reins from Bannock's slackening fingers.

Coe brought the stage in, holding Bannock up with one hand while driving with the other.

Bannock had survived the bad wound,

though Coe always believed it hastened his ultimate death. Bannock had never been a well man after that day.

Coe snorted again as he walked along, thinking of Kincaid's threat of firing him. Kincaid didn't know it, but there was no way he could accomplish that. Myra would rip him apart if Kincaid even dared to suggest it.

Coe debated upon talking to Myra about tonight's incident in the saloon, then decided against it. It was late, and Myra would probably be asleep. He would wait and give his version of it in the morning. He was smart enough not to stack the cards against himself by picking the wrong time.

He yawned prodigiously as he entered Crawford's little house at the edge of town. He was so damned sleepy. Maybe he hadn't reached his capacity tonight, but he was too damned close to it.

He cursed the door's creaking as he opened it. It was dark inside, and he kept bumping into objects. If Crawford was asleep, he wouldn't be for long at this rate.

Coe's boots against the floor sounded as loud as a six-team span of mules crossing a wooden bridge. Should have taken them off outside, he thought. He entered the bedroom and bumped into a chair. The impact sent it clattering across the floor.

'Why don't you light the lamp?' a voice snapped, 'and quit bumping into everything?'

Coe's tone showed how contrite he was. 'Bill, I was only trying to keep from waking you.'

'Then you didn't succeed,' Crawford said sourly.

Coe was careful lifting the globe from the lamp. He didn't want to drop and break it. They must be making lamp wicks smaller, for the first match burned down and seared his fingers before he could touch it to the wick.

He used two more matches before he lit the lamp. The strengthening illumination chased the shadows into the corners of the room.

Coe stared owl-eyed at Crawford, not sure whether or not to grin at him. Crawford was in bed, propped up on an elbow.

'Bill, I sure didn't want to wake you up.'

Crawford grinned wryly. 'Then you failed. I heard you open the front door; I heard every step you took.'

'Your leg hurting that much?' Coe asked in instant alarm.

Crawford made an impatient movement of his hands. 'No,' he growled. 'I just couldn't sleep.' His eyes could bore like augers. 'You're home pretty early for you. What happened? Did you run out of money or get into trouble?'

Coe pulled his remaining money from his pocket. 'I'm not broke,' he crowed. That should take Crawford's attention off the second part of his question.

'How much have you got there?' Crawford asked with ominous calm.

Coe counted his money twice to be sure of the figure.

'Nine dollars,' he announced triumphantly. His grin broadened. Crawford was always saying he couldn't keep money.

Crawford sat bolt upright. 'Nine dollars,' he said incredulously. 'You had almost a hundred dollars when you left that poker game. What did you do with it?'

Coe scratched his head. He never worried about money. How was he supposed to keep track of something so unimportant?

'I bought a few drinks,' Coe said frowning. 'I gave Flora a few tips.'

'A few,' Crawford snorted. 'From what I saw, you gave her at least twenty dollars.'

'I guess I did,' Coe admitted. His face

brightened. 'Oh, yes, I loaned Simmons ten dollars when you stepped away from the table for a few minutes.'

'Oh good God,' Crawford said in despair. 'You can kiss that money good-by.' He cut off Coe's protest by saying fiercely, 'You've loaned Simmons money before. Has he ever paid any of it back?'

'No,' Coe said, looking sheepish. 'But he will one of these days. I know he will.'

'What do you use for brains?' Crawford said savagely. 'All right. What did you do with the rest of the money?'

Coe scratched his head again. Crawford was always asking such bothersome questions. 'You know I must have spent some of it foolishly,' Coe said and grinned.

Crawford swore at him with feeling. He leveled an accusing finger at Coe. 'Why, damn it. This time, you promised me you'd put some of that money in the bank. For the first time in your life, you were going to start building a little security. I wanted to believe you so bad I didn't use any sense. I should have taken that money from you. How old do you have to get before you do some thinking?'

Coe patiently endured the tirade. He would take just about anything from this man. Nothing could ever make him forgot what he owed Bill Crawford. He was twelve years old when he first saw Crawford. He had stepped into water over his head, and he didn't know how to swim. Crawford had pulled him out of that deep hole, saving his life. After that, Coe had followed Crawford around like a shadow until Crawford became irritated enough to yell at him.

Coe never paid any attention to what Crawford said. Crawford sounded tough, but it wasn't the real man talking. Coe had hung around Crawford's saddle shop after that, anxious to do any little errand he could for Bill. After a year, Crawford said grudgingly, 'If you're going to hang around and work, I guess I better pay you.'

Coe tried to refuse the payment, and Crawford had yelled at him. 'You're as big a fool as your old man. You've earned this money. Take it. My God, didn't Jake ever teach you anything?' He stabbed a finger at Coe. 'Don't you give any of it to Jake. He'd only drink it up.'

Crawford yelled a lot, and he always sounded mad, but Coe adored him. Coe's father died when he was fourteen. Maybe it was the hard drinking that put Jake into an early grave. Crawford was one of the few people who attended the funeral. After it was over Crawford said gruffly, 'You better move in with me until we can figure out something else.'

Coe moved in with him. Nothing was ever said about him moving out, so he had stayed. When he was sixteen, Coe had gone to work for the Bannocks. Coe suspected it was a relief to Crawford to be able to stop paying him anything. Crawford's shop was barely making its way.

Crawford had an uncanny perception that sometimes frightened Coe. He could look into a man's head and see what was going on in there.

'What trouble did you get into?' Crawford asked quietly.

Coe made a vague gesture. 'No trouble.' He tried to work up a righteous indignation. 'Do you think I have to get into trouble every time I have a few drinks?'

'Damned close to it,' Crawford said dryly. 'You came back with money in your pocket. That means you ran into trouble that made you leave. What was it?'

Coe sighed. There was no use trying to keep anything hidden from Crawford. 'No real trouble,' he said weakly. 'Kincaid came in and raised hell about me drinking. One

37

word led to another, and he swung at me.' Coe rubbed his cheek in reflective memory of the sting there. 'I guess he didn't really hurt me. But I knocked him down.'

Crawford's eyes were round. 'Jesus Christ,' he whispered. 'He fired you.'

Coe stared at him, honestly puzzled. How did Crawford know that?

Crawford swore helplessly. 'It couldn't figure any other way. Kincaid couldn't whip you physically. He did the only thing left to him. He fired you.'

Coe shrugged with elaborate disdain. 'It won't stick. Myra wouldn't stand for it.'

Crawford threw up his hands in defeat. 'Coe, what's it going to take to change you? For years, I've been trying to get you to look ahead, to plan. But you just go along as though tomorrow doesn't exist.'

'It don't,' Coe said and grinned. 'Not until it gets here.'

Honest bafflement was in Crawford's eyes. 'Have you ever thought of what could happen to your job if something happened to Myra?'

Coe was beginning to get angry. Crawford was always nipping at his ass like a feisty little terrier annoying a big old hound dog. One snap, and the feisty terrier wouldn't be

38

any more. Coe instantly retracted that thought. He wouldn't have anything happen to Bill Crawford for anything in the world.

Coe sat down on his bed to tug off his boots. They came off easily. Crawford was always saying he couldn't take advice. These boots were proof of how wrong Crawford was. Jake had always told him to wear loose boots.

Coe undressed, blew out the lamp, and climbed into bed. 'Bill,' he said gently, 'I think you enjoy fretting over me. You're always yelling about the bad things that can happen to me. Have they happened yet?' he finished reasonably.

Crawford didn't answer his question. Maybe he had shut Crawford up this time. He turned over and was instantly asleep.

Crawford stared bleakly into the darkness as he listened to the soft snoring. Coe was going the same road his father traveled, but Coe couldn't see it. Jake was another happy-go-lucky individual, and he had literally drunk himself to an early death. Crawford groaned in soft anguish at the thought of Coe ending the same way.

CHAPTER THREE

Jett Kincaid stomped out of Brown's saloon in a high rage. Everybody there had been on Coe's side. He had seen it on their faces. Nobody had offered him a hand in getting up, or had wanted to listen to his angry explanations. Damn them all. He would show them Coe couldn't get away with this. This time, he would insist Myra back him up. He would demand that Coe be fired.

Kincaid couldn't make the thought as convincing as he wished. He knew how Myra felt about Coe. But she would go along with him, or– Kincaid stopped in helpless frustration. That was only angry bluster unless he could find something to give the threat solid basis. He could walk out on her, he thought petulantly.

He slammed his fist into a palm. That was a hollow threat and he knew it. He had no intention of walking away and leaving what he had. Marrying Myra was the best thing that had ever happened to him. Not because he loved her but for all the material advantages she brought him. The stage line was a thriving business, and for the first time in Kincaid's life, he could have just about anything he wanted. But he lacked one thing he wanted so desperately – he lacked authority. He wanted to be known as the boss of Bannock Stage Lines, not just as Myra's husband. He admitted a few times his judgment had been bad, for he had seen the derision in some of the help's eyes when he gave an order. Those times had been as bitter as gall, and he had to swallow it. He had gone ahead and foolishly insisted that his orders be carried out. Then, the derision screamed at him. Unless Myra backed up his orders, his authority was as leaky as a sieve. Too many times, Myra had stepped in and countermanded his instructions. Coe had that same derision in his eyes tonight.

Goddamn it, Kincaid thought frantically. This time, she's got to listen to me. Too many people had seen him attempt to fire Coe. The props under his ego were too shaky now. If Coe wasn't fired, the whole town would know that Kincaid was only a hollow shell.

His step quickened as he debated upon what he was going to do. Should he go home and tell Myra what had happened? He shook his head against that idea. The timing would be bad. Sometimes, Myra could have a waspish temper when she awakened out of a sound sleep. No, he would wait until morning to broach the subject. He cursed as he remembered how she had been the first months of their marriage. She would awaken dewey-eyed and trembling as she awaited his touch. It wasn't that way any more. He had caught her too often looking at him with speculative eyes as though she sought a solution to a problem. Too many times, he had heard her sigh when she didn't know he was around. Something had happened to her, and he didn't have the slightest idea of what it was.

He turned toward his office, too wide awake to think of going home. He wanted to be alone with his thoughts, aided by a few drinks of good whiskey. The bottle in his desk drawer was the answer to the latter part, for he could afford to drink only the best. He wasn't so sure how his thoughts would come out.

'Damn you, Coe,' he muttered as he unlocked the door, 'I'll fix you yet.' Right now, he knew that was a childish scream of defiance, but he would change that.

He walked into his office and settled in his

comfortable chair. He pulled out the bottle and drew out the cork. His eyes lighted with appreciation as he sipped the whiskey. It was as smooth as silk with a warm authority that didn't hit him all at once. He wished everything went as smoothly for him.

He scowled as he thought he heard a footstep in the outer office. Had he locked the door after he entered? He couldn't remember. His feet slid off of the desk and hit the floor with a thud. He better go investigate.

He checked himself after a couple of steps. That could be Myra. His face turned sulky. Her being down here this late could only mean one thing; that she had heard about his run-in with Coe. If that was so, it meant that she had gotten somebody's version of what happened. If so, her mind could be made up.

Kincaid muttered a soft oath. He knew how stubborn she could be. He stood there, listening to the soft patter of feminine feet crossing the outer office. He was in no mood to take much opposition tonight. His face and pride hurt in equal proportions. If Myra jumped him tonight, he would– Again, he fumbled for a finish to the thought. It seemed as though he could start

43

them and couldn't come up with a finish.

His jaw sagged as Belle Thomas came into the room. He had seen her last night; he certainly hadn't expected to see her tonight and particularly not here.

He put his apprehension into words. 'My God, Belle, you shouldn't be here.' He felt the sweat break out on him as he thought of Myra walking in and finding Belle here.

Belle pouted at his tone. 'Don't you want me, Jett? Last night, you gave me the impression you did at any time, any place. I saw you come in and followed you. The door was unlocked, I thought you'd welcome me.' She shrugged those expressive shoulders. 'I see I was wrong.'

She was a stunning brunette with a face that all women envied, and a figure that matched the face. Either was enough to drive a man out of his mind.

She turned to leave, and Kincaid sprang forward, seizing her hand. Last night came vividly back to him, and he groaned inwardly. He had known her a dozen times, and each was more overwhelming than the preceding one. She was a complete woman, and she gave him full satisfaction. He had never known anybody like her. She was a flame that kept burning brighter and

44

brighter, and he was sure it would never go out.

He looked at the low-cut line of her dress, remembering how those breasts looked last night. Her reputation wasn't the best in Tucson, and women avoided, or sniffed openly at her. She owned the most notorious house in Tucson, and her price was high. Kincaid was willing to pay that price. He knew all the other things, and it didn't matter. If it was only a simulated passion he bought, he didn't care. She gave him what no other woman had been able to; she left him drained but at peace, and content.

He threw aside all caution, burying his fear that Myra might walk in. Nothing mattered but that Belle was here.

He drew her to him. 'Belle, you know better than that.' His voice was hoarse, his breathing rapid and strained.

Belle laughed with undisguised pleasure. She was all animal, and only outward signs of her power over males interested her.

'For a moment, I was wondering,' she said and kissed him.

She never did anything halfway. It needed only a small stirring of last night's ashes to bring the flame into a full roaring fire.

He was almost sobbing as he lifted his

head. Caution was the furthest thing from his mind. He kissed her cheek, her jawline. His lips slid down the satiny column of her neck and moved farther down the cleft between her breasts.

She laughed again, her hands pressing his head closer to her.

'Well,' a cold, remote voice said, 'this is an interesting sight.'

CHAPTER FOUR

Myra Kincaid walked slowly down the street. She was depressed and tired from her visit with Neva Mallory. Hank Mallory had been one of Myra's stable hands. A kick from a horse had crushed his skull. Myra tried several times to console Neva and was unsuccessful. Even a gift of money couldn't begin to replace Neva's terrible loss.

Myra sighed and shook her head. She vowed she would never again visit Neva. She patiently listened to Neva going over all the details she covered before. She made it sound as though her marriage to Hank Mallory was one of the great loves of all time. Myra knew that wasn't true. Mallory was a hard drinker and slovenly in everything he did. Myra heard talk that Mallory laid rough hands on his wife. She paid little attention to such talk. A town was rife with such rumors, and too many malicious tongues liked to pick up any gossip and pass it on.

You're getting cynical, Myra accused

herself. But too many widows went the same way Neva was going. Mallory's funeral was the outstanding event in an otherwise drab life. It focused public attention on her, and she milked that attention for everything she could.

That won't last long, Neva, Myra thought. Soon, people will be running from you. There's only a certain amount of sympathy in people. When that's gone, there's no more. Neva constantly wailed her loneliness. Neva would really know loneliness when people started avoiding her.

Myra shook her head. There was that cynicism again. Like Neva, she was changing too, and not for the better. She knew she was pulling a hard shell about her, but seemed unable to do anything about it. Oh, Jett, a lonely, inner voice wailed.

She was a plain woman and well aware of it. Long ago, she had accepted the fact she would never be attractive to the opposite sex. She tried to erase the feeling of loss by more and more application to the business. When Brad died, she was as fully capable as he. Her eyes stung with unshed tears as she remembered Brad's last words. 'A year ago, I would have worried about you. But not now. Honey, you're going to be all right.'

She angrily shook her head. Brad was seldom wrong, but his last words were. Nothing was right for her.

Her one redeeming feature was her eyes. They were large and magnificent. For a while after her marriage to Jett, people had commented upon how she had blossomed out, that her eyes were luminous. She knew the cause of the change. It was Jett Kincaid. How well she remembered the eagerness with which she awaited his touch. But that eagerness faded rapidly. It was all gone before the first year of her marriage was over. She was a sane, practical woman, and her honesty let her accept facts honestly. She didn't have enough to hold Jett's interest. Now, she plodded through the dull days, wrapping business around her in substitute. It wasn't enough, though she rarely admitted it, even to herself. You're a fool, Myra Kincaid, she thought sharply. You're wallowing in self-pity.

She frowned as she turned a corner. A light in the Bannock Stage building was on, and at this hour, that was unusual. Jett hadn't shown enough interest in the business to work long hours. He was only interested in what the business brought him, not in working for it.

49

Jett had to be here, for she had the only other key to the office. Could he be changing? She would not allow the eagerness to come alive again. She had tripped over that vulnerability before. She would not allow it to happen again.

Her frown deepened as she opened the door. If Jett was here, he was careless in leaving the door unlocked. She would have to tell him about that. She sighed. It seemed all she did lately was admonish him for his lack in everything.

She crossed the outer office, thinking she heard the murmur of voices coming from Jett's office.

She stopped in the doorway, her heart plummeting at what she saw. She wanted to scream and rave, and she curbed the impulse. Oh, she had heard gossip of Jett's straying interest, but she wouldn't allow herself to give the gossip any credence. Her doubts were all removed by the scene before her.

'Well,' she said in a cold, remote voice, 'this is an interesting sight.'

Jett and Belle sprang apart, their faces a study in guilt. Belle recovered first, for she laughed softly. Jett's face was a mottled red and white, and he stammered, trying to find an adequate explanation.

'Myra, this isn't what you think it is. I – I only–' His tongue grew thicker, and he couldn't go on.

Myra's eyes were filled with undisguised contempt. 'Can't you go ahead and talk, Jett?' she mocked. She prided herself on her control, but it was slipping rapidly away. 'Don't try to lie, Jett. I've got eyes.' Her face burned with her humiliation, but she kept her head proudly erect. 'I heard rumors of this, but I refused to believe. Jett, I gave you every doubt. I was a fool.'

Belle laughed again, and Myra's face flamed at the insolence.

'Get this tramp out of my office,' Myra cried. Her voice was growing shrill. She was very near the breaking point.

Belle straightened out her dress, and her laughter was the sound of triumph. 'I'll see you again, honey,' she said and strolled out of the office.

Myra kept that icy control, though every impulse was to claw this bitch until she ran blood.

Jett couldn't meet Myra's eyes. He pulled at his fingers as he looked everywhere but at her. 'Myra, I can explain all this,' he said hoarsely. 'It's not as bad as it seems.'

'Go ahead, Jett,' Myra said, the contempt naked in her eyes. 'I want to hear you explain this away.'

His face burned as he made a half-dozen false starts. With each start, he dug the hole in which he stood, ever deeper.

'Oh, stop it,' Myra said wearily. 'Do you think I'm an utter fool?'

He mistook the weariness in her voice as a sign that she could no longer stand to hold out against him. 'No, I'm the damned fool, Myra. I gave way momentarily to the weakness that's in all men. I was working when Belle wandered in. I must have forgotten to lock the door. I'd had a couple of drinks, and I welcomed the excuse to let up, to talk to somebody for a few minutes.' His face was humble, and this time he managed to look squarely at Myra. 'I'm ashamed of my weakness, but she is an attractive woman. Maybe I was too tired, or maybe it was the perfume she was wearing.' His smile grew more stable. Myra was listening, and she had made no protest yet. Those were signs that she wanted to believe him. His confidence grew. His dominance over her might have been weakened by that little incident with Belle, but it wasn't ruptured completely.

He moved a step nearer, reaching out a

hand. 'Myra,' he said earnestly. 'I don't have to promise you it will never happen again.' He chuckled ruefully. 'My God, if you knew how scared I was when I saw you standing there. The only thing I could think of was that I'd lost you. You don't think I'd ever risk that again, do you?' He shook his head in self-reproach, but inwardly he felt like laughing. She had never been able to resist him. 'You have a right to be upset, Myra. Let's go home. We'll talk about this in the morning when both of us are calm.'

She slapped at his hand and retreated. Her face was contorted with raw passion. He still considered her as putty in his hands. Jett didn't realize he had lost his hold on her months ago.

'Don't touch me,' she said. Her voice rose with each word until soon she would be screaming at him. That would be the final indignity, breaking down completely before him.

She blinked several times, afraid she wouldn't be able to control the telltale tears. 'On top of everything else wrong with you, Jett, you're a contemptible liar. You're not going home with me tonight, or any other time. You'll find your clothes on the porch. Get your personal things out of this office and don't ever come back.'

He stared at her aghast, feeling so physically ill that he thought he would vomit. The thought of losing everything he'd struggled to gain made his head reel. His mouth was dry, and his tongue was unable to move. He licked his lips several times before he could speak.

'You can't mean that, Myra. You can't throw away everything we have.'

'Oh, can't I?' Her voice was icily remote. 'I'm going to Prescott in the morning. Don't be here when I return, or I'll have Coe or one of the other boys throw you out. If you don't think I mean that, just try me.'

She turned and walked toward the door, forcing herself to keep from running. The tears were beginning to come now, and they felt hot on her cheeks. She didn't turn her head as he called her name. He was still calling it as she stepped out of the building.

Sobs shook her body, and that lonely inner voice kept screaming, Oh, Jett. She angrily tossed her head, berating her weakness. Nothing would change her, not after what she had seen. She would have to get used to the loneliness.

Her steps quickened until she was almost running. She forced herself to slow down before she broke into absolute flight. A thought stopped her. She hadn't asked Jett for his key.

She resisted the impulse to go back and demand it. Keeping the key would do him no good. Besides, she could not stand looking at him again. She resumed a more normal pace. If anybody passed her now, she thought they wouldn't be able to see the turmoil within her. At least, she hoped they wouldn't. The lonely, inner voice wailed again, Oh, Jett.

Kincaid stood there stunned. He couldn't believe this had happened. Even now, he was tempted to run after Myra and force her to listen. The memory of the contempt in those blazing eyes checked him. Even his conceit couldn't go up against that contempt.

He raved and swore at the top of his voice, pacing the office as he yelled. He cursed Myra with every oath at his command, and he included Belle. Damn Belle! None of this would have happened if she hadn't come in here tonight. He thought of Myra's threat to have Coe throw him out, and that made matters worse. Coe would welcome the chance to do just that.

The wildness grew until he was frantic

with his helplessness. 'Goddamn them all,' he screamed at the top of his voice.

Sound wasn't what he needed; he needed action, violent action. He swept his arm across the desk top, sending the objects on it flying. He picked up the chair and raised it over his head. He would smash up this office until Myra wouldn't recognize it.

He slowly lowered the chair as a thread of sanity filtered through his thinking. He needed that violence, but it wouldn't do him any good. He didn't know how vindictive Myra was, but he could well imagine that in retaliation for wrecking this office, she could send Coe after him. He sank limply into the chair, burying his face in his hands. He recalled how many people heard his threat of firing Coe. Now, he didn't have a job. He groaned miserably at the thought of being the laughingstock of Tucson.

His hand shook as he poured himself a drink. He needed that to soothe his jangled nerves. He gulped down the drink and poured himself another. How could a man stand on the pinnacle one moment, then in the next be on a toboggan slide headed straight for the bottom?

He started to pour another drink, then set the bottle down without filling his glass.

Drinking himself into maudlin self-pity wouldn't solve anything. If he was going to save anything out of this mess, he had to think.

He leaned back in his chair and closed his eyes. Thoughts were little devils, racing about in his head, screaming obscenities at him. He couldn't get hold of anything solid.

Could he talk to Myra in the morning? He tried to build that up into a full-fledged hope, then disconsolately shook his head. He knew Myra well enough to know he couldn't get within yelling distance of her. He had stamped on her pride, and a woman never forgave that.

He beat at the desk in impotent rage. 'Think, damn you,' he cursed himself. Myra had said something about going to Prescott in the morning. Oh God, if there was some way he could make sure she never came back. If something did happen to her, this business would be all his. His head lifted, and an ugly gleam filled his eyes. He doubted that Myra would talk about what happened tonight. That was between husband and wife: she would never talk of something that intimate. The thought grew in his mind until he wanted to shout under its stimulation. If she didn't return, he would be left as the grieving husband, but the business would belong to him. His hands clenched so tightly they ached. Oh God, if an accident occurred that wiped out the stage. Including Coe Dahmer, he thought viciously. That would be an added bonus.

What could cause that accident? He breathed harder as he thought of one thing after another. No violence, he warned himself, for violence left telltale evidence. This had to be just an ordinary accident without arousing anybody's suspicions.

Kincaid's eyes widened as he thought of how that accident could be caused. 'That could be it,' he muttered, jumping to his feet. It wouldn't be foolproof, but if everything turned out in his favor, it could work.

He hurried out into the stable area, his mind pulling and prying at the hidden flaws in his scheme. He could see all the imponderables, and it would take excellent timing to work. He would have no guarantee that the accident would be conclusive. Myra could escape with no more than a shaking up, or a minor injury. But at least, it would be a positive action. He wouldn't be sitting around bemoaning his rotten fortune.

The stage to Prescott was all ready. Kincaid grunted sourly at its shining splendor.

This was another of Myra's nonsense ideas. She insisted no stage pulled out of a depot until it was washed, or at least dusted off. Kincaid shook his head in disgust. She also ordered the stages painted, preferably every year but never going beyond two. She maintained that it built confidence in the traveling public. Kincaid had never been able to argue her out of that fool stand. If somebody wanted to go some place, they didn't give a damn what the stage looked like.

He looked at the stage a long moment, and the shaky hollow in his stomach grew.

Well, get ahead with it, he snarled to himself, or turn and walk away.

He looked all around him, and the night guard wasn't in sight. Probably he's slipped out for a drink, Kincaid concluded.

He hurried to the tool house, found the wrench he needed, and came back, his heart pounding. He fitted the wrench to a rear-wheel nut and unscrewed it, stopping before the nut was completely off.

He laid the wrench on the ground and tried the nut with his fingers. It turned easily. Was it too loose? An agony of indecision wracked him. This was where one of the imponderables came in. He wanted the nut to stay on until Brady's Grade was reached.

The road narrowed there until the right hand side of the stage hung over the sharp drop. He tightened the nut back with his fingers. This would be asking for a small miracle of timing, but dammit, after his rotten luck, he deserved a break. Oh God, let the nut stay on until Coe reaches the grade. Kincaid shivered at the enormity of praying for something like that.

He unloosened the nut a half turn. There was no doubt it would work off during the stage's running. But where, was the big question. He shivered again. There was nothing else he could do.

He heard footsteps and straightened. The night guard was coming this way. At the moment, Sam Cummings' figure was only an indistinct blob, but Kincaid knew he couldn't be caught around the stage, particularly with a wrench in his hand. He scooped up the wrench and hurried to the tool house. He tossed the wrench inside, not having enough time to return it to its proper place, and closed the door.

'Hold it,' Cummings yelled. 'What are you doing there?' He broke into an awkward run, his increased years hampering him.

'Hello, Cummings,' Kincaid said. His pounding heart made it difficult for him to keep his voice easy and normal.

Cummings came up and peered at him. 'Oh, it's you, Mr Kincaid. I didn't recognize you. For a minute, you had me worried. I thought I had some petty thief on my hands.' He shook his head, the gesture saying how foolish his worry had been. He was a tired, old man, his face lined from age. Night guarding was about the only job Cummings could hold.

'I was just checking over things,' Kincaid said. His breathing was almost back to normal, and he could laugh easily. 'With you on the job, I should have known that everything was under control.'

Cummings grinned, pleased at Kincaid's praise. 'I try to keep it that way, Mr Kincaid.'

Kincaid whacked him on the shoulder. 'Sure, you do, Cummings. Just don't ever let down.'

'Yes, sir,' Cummings responded.

Kincaid walked away without looking back. He had done everything he could. All he could do now was to hope that luck was on his side.

CHAPTER FIVE

Coe struck at the hand that insisted on roughly shaking him awake. 'Let me sleep,' he mumbled.

The offending hand came back and grabbed his shoulder. A voice added its torment to the shaking. 'Come on, Coe. Wake up. Or do you intend to miss your run?'

The question jolted Coe into awareness. He opened his eyes, then hastily shut them, wincing at the brilliant impact of the light from the lamp. He cautiously opened one eye at a time, to steel himself against the light's onslaught. It was only a coal-oil lamp. It shouldn't be giving out this much light.

Crawford had said something about Coe missing his run. That filled Coe with indignation. Nobody would ever accuse him of being too hungover to take his run.

He sat up abruptly and instantly regretted the rashness of the movement. His head threatened to pound off his shoulders. Cradling his head in his hands Coe sank back to the cushion of his pillow. He fully expected to feel his head expanding and contracting under the merciless hammering inside it.

'God, I feel awful,' he groaned. He squinted up at Crawford's unfeeling face. 'Damn it, Bill,' he said plaintively, 'I haven't had an hour's sleep.'

'A little more than that,' Crawford said without sympathy. 'Feel bad, do you?' Crawford's short burst of laughter was a cruel sound. 'You earned it. Do you want me to go down and tell them you can't make it?'

Coe sat up again, ignoring the renewed fury that tried to tear his head apart. 'You know better than that. You've never seen the day when I had to beg off.' He didn't say that with as much conviction as he wished. He never felt worse. His stomach was a seething, boiling caldron. Every time it turned over, he was sure he was going to lose everything. The taste in his mouth gagged him. He thought grimly, You're damned close to begging off. Another drink last night, and you wouldn't have been able to crawl. He tried to grin whimsically as a thought occurred to him. Maybe he owed Kincaid a favor for stopping him last night. He almost wished Kincaid had the authority to fire him and make it stick. Then he

63

wouldn't have to go through this torment.

'Then you better get moving,' Crawford said with the same cruel lack of feeling. 'You haven't got much time left.'

Coe climbed out of bed and staggered to the dresser. He had to focus his bleary eyes to see the watch laying there. He groaned at what he saw. The stage was supposed to pull out in a half hour. He wanted to swear at the remorseless hands of the watch. He was in no shape to move in a hurry this morning, but those damned hands wouldn't stop. With each tiny movement, they were tearing him apart.

He rubbed his knuckles over his beard stubble. Myra would raise pure hell if she saw him looking like this. She demanded that her drivers look respectable. Now, he had to shave, and he wasn't sure his hand was steady enough to guide a razor.

'Why didn't you call me earlier?' he yelped.

Crawford's grin was malicious. 'I've been trying to get you up for the last hour. I was about ready to tell you to go to hell when you finally mumbled and opened your eyes.'

'I've got to shave,' Coe said. The sense of urgency was mounting, driving him frantic.

'Maybe it'll make you look a little better,'

Crawford observed. 'Though I doubt it.'

Coe swore feebly at him. Why didn't Crawford let him alone?

'Bill, is there any hot water?'

'At this hour of the morning?' Crawford hooted.

Coe moaned. The devil was in charge of this morning. His beard was tough. Without hot water to soften it, he would go through hell.

He dressed as fast as he could, his shaky hands making the task doubly hard. He walked into the kitchen and poured cold water into a pan. He looked at his bloodshot eyes in the mirror and shuddered.

'I look like death warmed over,' he said with a feeble attempt at humor.

'Worse than that,' Crawford said in brutal agreement. 'Coe, when are you going to stop abusing yourself?'

Coe hung onto his temper by his fingernails. If Crawford didn't shut up, Coe was going to have to fly into him. 'I'll manage,' he said through tight lips.

Perhaps Coe's tone was enough warning to Crawford, for he sighed and fell silent.

Coe nerved himself to stand the touch of the cold water he splashed into his face. The lather wouldn't build up enough to protect his skin. He gritted his teeth and started shaving.

Coe yelped before he finished the first swath of the blade and stared at the welling red on his cheek. Oh, goddamn it! He'd cut himself. He cut himself three more times before he finished the miserable chore. He tore little bits of paper, moistened and plastered them against the wounds.

'Damn it,' he said bitterly. 'I'm bleeding to death.'

'You were before you started shaving,' Crawford said caustically. 'Cutting yourself only hastened it. I thought you were bleeding to death through your eyes.'

'You're a very funny man,' Coe said sourly. 'Remind me to laugh sometime.' He scowled at his reflection in the mirror. His face looked like a botched-up butchering job on a hog. 'What kind of a day is it, Bill?'

'Raw and foggy,' Crawford answered. 'You'd better wear your sheepskin.'

Coe groaned. Crawford's summary of the day fitted in with everything else. Tucson didn't get many days like this in the winter, but when one came along, its savage contrast was like vicious fangs ripping a man apart.

'I'll go get my coat,' Coe said unhappily.

66

This kind of a day was hard enough to bear even when he was in good shape. Right now, he was about as far from that as he could get.

He pulled his sheepskin out of a closet and slipped into it. Just thinking of sitting high up there, with the wind tearing at him, made his teeth chatter.

He had the cure for that misery, in the top drawer of his chest. He opened the drawer, pawed under a stack of clothing, looked guiltily around him, then slipped the pint bottle into his coat pocket. He sure didn't want Crawford seeing that bottle, or he would have to listen to more jawing.

Crawford was waiting for him at the front door. 'Coe, you're going to stop and get some breakfast, aren't you?'

Just the thought of food set Coe's teeth on edge and made him wince. 'I haven't got the time, Bill. I'll be all right.'

All the sharpness was gone out of Crawford's voice. A hand rested briefly on Coe's shoulder. 'Coe, you watch yourself good. You hear me?'

Coe gave him a genuine smile. 'I hear you, Bill.' He touched the brim of his hat and walked outside. A remnant of the smile remained on his face. That irascible, old cuss. Crawford tried to hide his concern, but he worried about Coe. His sharp tongue did a poor job of covering up his concern.

'You needn't worry, Bill,' Coe muttered. Hell, hadn't he proven by now that he could take care of himself?

He turned the sheepskin collar up around his ears. The fog wasn't as bad as some he'd seen, but it was bad enough. The sun was just rising, and its watery rays so far were ineffectual against the gray shroud. But the wind was strengthening. That would blow out the fog soon. The wind would help on one hand and hurt on the other, for it drove the chill through Coe. Even the sheepskin seemed unable to do much more than blunt the wind's teeth.

He knew what he needed. A glance about him assured him no one was on the street. At this hour, no sane man would be out if it wasn't necessary. He stepped into a doorway and pulled out the bottle. The cork came out with a soft, sucking sound, and Coe raised the bottle to his mouth. He hesitated momentarily, and he knew what he was doing. The hesitation was a bracing against the savage assault on his mouth, throat and stomach.

Coe drank long, forcing his throat to make

swallow after swallow. He lowered the bottle and shuddered. This morning, the whiskey tasted as cold as ice water.

He was right in expecting that savage assault, for he choked and gagged. A severe fit of coughing seized him, and he waited for the paroxysm to pass. The whiskey hit his abused stomach and punched around with brutal authority.

Coe wiped the water out of his eyes. He could feel the warmth of the whiskey slowly steal through him. 'The hair of the dog that bit me,' Coe muttered. At the moment, he was doubtful of the effectiveness of the cure.

He took a second drink, and it didn't make him nearly as nauseous as the first. The heat within his body increased. By God, he was going to live.

Coe debated upon taking another drink, then decided against it. He recorked the bottle and slipped it into his outer pocket. He had a long day ahead; he would need the drink worse later on.

He turned a corner and strode hurriedly toward the depot. The stage was drawn up before it, the teams in harness. Myra walked up and down beside the stage, the positive thud of her heels against the ground showing how upset she was.

Coe grinned twistedly. He had cut it pretty fine. He came up to her and said, 'Morning, Myra.' He was concerned about his run-in with Kincaid last night and didn't quite know how to approach the subject. Don't be a damned fool, he admonished himself. Kincaid isn't around. Maybe he hadn't time to say anything about it to her.

Myra whirled at the sound of Coe's voice, and her eyes scanned his face. She knows something about it, he thought mournfully. She's mad. But he still waited for her to open the subject. He didn't know what Kincaid told her, or how much he had elaborated. Coe needed some facts before he even tried to defend himself.

'You're late,' she snapped. 'I was almost ready to call another driver.'

'Shucks, Myra,' Coe said lightly, 'you didn't have cause to worry. Did you ever know me to miss a run?' He tried to keep his relief from showing on his face. She seemed upset all right, but last night's episode didn't seem to be the cause.

'Have you been drinking, Coe?' Her tone had a crackle in it.

His relief vanished. She knew something about last night, or she wouldn't have asked that question.

70

'I had a few last night,' he admitted cautiously, keeping his face turned from her. He didn't want the fan of his breath reaching her. Myra didn't approve of her drivers drinking. He thought mournfully that maybe Kincaid's brag of firing him was coming true. Myra was ready to back up her husband. She was only letting Coe dig his own grave before she shoved him into it.

'Did you ever know me to take more than I can handle, Myra? I don't care what Jett said. He's got it wrong.'

Her eyes narrowed. 'You saw him last night?'

He groaned in agony. She knew he had. There was cat in her, and he was the mouse. She was playing with him before she made the final slash of her paw.

'I did,' he admitted ruefully. 'In Charley Brown's saloon.'

Her breathing seemed to come with more difficulty. Coe couldn't remember seeing her more agitated.

'Was he alone?' she asked, then bit her lower lip. 'No,' she said decisively, 'I don't want to hear about it.'

Coe didn't let his bewilderment show. Both of them were talking and thinking of two different things. His relief flooded back.

Whatever bothered her didn't seem to have anything to do with his drinking.

'Sure, Myra,' he said.

'Only two passengers this morning, Coe,' she said crisply. 'It's time to be going.' She turned to climb into the stage.

He couldn't keep the bafflement from his voice. 'You're going this morning, Myra?' he asked stupidly. Hell, he could see that she was.

She looked at him over her shoulder. 'I am. To Prescott. I've been dissatisfied with the way the depot there is being run.' Her smile was bleak. 'Maybe I'll fire a manager before this day is out.'

Coe helped her up and closed the door behind her. He wasn't thinking very clearly this morning. Was she still playing with her mouse? Was she only going along to check up to see how bad his driving was? That could be the answer. Kincaid had built up what bad shape he was in. All Myra had to do was watch him drive this morning. Maybe Coe's firing waited for him a little down the road.

He shook his head in bewilderment. He didn't understand this at all. Myra wasn't a devious woman, and he had never known her to lie. But it looked as though all his prior estimations of her were being whipped to pieces.

Myra stuck her head through the window. 'Are you going to stand there all morning?' she demanded. For the first time, he got a close look at her eyes. They were red and swollen. That added to his confusion. Hard and prolonged crying was the only thing he knew that would produce such results.

'No,' he replied and climbed up to the driver's seat. He kicked off the brakes and snapped the reins on the wheelers' rumps. 'Ho,' he yelled sharply. His resentment built steadily. She knew what kind of a driver he was; she didn't have to come along to check on him. He was fully convinced she and Kincaid had set this up. Well, he'd show them. He'd stuff the carefully baited trap back down their throats.

He had the teams in full stride before he reached the outskirts of town. He would not only meet the schedule, he would beat it. By God, she would be embarrassed and sorry, then.

His steadily growing anger fortified him against the lash of the wind. He drove four miles before he even thought of the bottle in his pocket. The fog was almost dissipated, but he needed something against that wind.

73

The effect of the earlier drinks had worn off, and he needed another to replenish their power. He turned his head to glare at the stage roof. Myra was under it, and he hoped she was enjoying her ride. Damn it, he wasn't a child that needed nursing.

He caught motion behind him before he looked back to his driving. A rider was a good distance behind him, too far to make out who it was. Coe shrugged away the problem of the rider's identity. Whoever it was, he would probably pass the stage before Brady's Grade or shortly after.

Coe drove another two miles, arguing against the temptation of the bottle in his pocket. He felt shaky, even though his hands on the reins were steady enough. Why not, he thought fiercely. Myra had no way of knowing if he took that drink. She might not agree with his viewpoint, but if another drink made him a steadier driver, it was all to her advantage.

He pulled out the bottle and took a long drink. Ah God, he needed that. He was feeling better before the drink was hardly down, and it re-established the clarity of his thinking. He glared back at the stage roof again. Myra might holler if she saw his bottle, but he wasn't giving her anything to complain about.

He caught another glimpse of the rider behind him. The gap between them hadn't lessened. Whoever the rider was, he sure wasn't in any hurry.

Coe refocused his attention on his driving. The drink lifted him so much that he even felt like singing. He grinned ruefully as he curbed the impulse. Wouldn't that startle Myra if she heard a burst of song coming from topside?

Coe never felt sharper, and he knew he was ahead of schedule. He snorted as he thought of the gloom hangers, who warned him about his drinking. There had never been a day when he'd been better with the reins.

Brady's Grade was a mile ahead. Coe transferred his thoughts to the grade. It was a wicked, narrow stretch of road, rising sharply before the road plunged down on the other side. He told himself he had nothing to worry about there. Hadn't he taken a hundred stages or more over that stretch? Just the same he couldn't erase the unease that nibbled at him.

He slowed the teams a little as he came into the grade. The natural upward tilt of the land would take off most of the remaining momentum. The teams would be barely moving when they reached the crest. There were two bad switchbacks before the road climbed to the top.

That damned unease was still riding him, and Coe went into the first switchback with more caution than usual. The inside of the stage almost scraped the hewed-out bank, and the outer side of the stage hung over the steep drop. It was enough to make any driver nervous. Coe swore at himself and spat contemptuously into empty space. Maybe the lack of sleep was making him edgy.

The stage lurched a little to the right just as Coe was straightening out on the switchback. He felt an instant and paralyzing flash of alarm. My God, Coe thought, my nerves are strung tight.

The alarm vanished as the stage continued moving, and he savagely rebuked his weakness.

His mouth opened wide with an unscreamed cry of fear. His tongue was plastered to the roof of his mouth, and he couldn't make a sound.

It seemed as though the right rear wheel of the stage just dropped away from the vehicle. The seat tilted higher and higher, and Coe scrambled to keep his place on the box.

Oh Jesus, he thought. I drove off the edge.

We're going over.

The inner side of the stage kept rising higher, and Coe dropped the reins. Nothing could keep the stage from going over, and he tried to jump before the stage started its long tumble toward the bottom of the slope.

He never made his jump. He was only half erect, and the stage was increasing its momentum. The rising seat slammed into him, knocking him off balance. He knew with conviction he wasn't going to get clear. He was thrown out into space. One mournful thought filled his head before he slammed into the ground. He wasn't nearly as sharp as he thought he was. His head hit first, and the whole heavens seemed to explode into a blinding burst of red fire, mercifully blotting out any following sensations.

He rolled over and over, but Coe didn't know a thing about it.

CHAPTER SIX

Kincaid pulled up at the spot where the stage went over. He felt a strange mixture of awe and jubilation as he stared at the wreckage at the bottom of the slope. The stage's twisting and tumbling had snapped off the shaft. One of the teams had been carried over the edge. Kincaid could see no life in those two animals. The two other teams had managed to tear free of the hampering harness and run on down the road. Kincaid supposed they would run until they were spent.

So far, he hadn't looked squarely at the stage, and he knew why. He was afraid he would see life stirring around the wreckage. At any moment, he expected to hear a faint cry for help.

A broken sob rattled in his throat, and he was beginning to shake; not from any remorse at what he had caused, but in fear that after coming this close, everything would be snatched from him. So far, the fates had been with him. The timing of the accident was perfect, and he couldn't have hand-picked a better spot for it to happen.

'Get on with it,' he said in a hoarse voice. He cursed himself for his weakness. Last night, with Myra kicking him out, he faced complete ruin. Now, he was on the verge of getting everything he wanted. He sucked in a deep breath, a fire starting in his eyes. If Myra was dead, the stage line would be his. How could she be alive after this drop?

He forced himself to study the wrecked stage, trying to take in every detail of the vehicle. From this height, it looked like a broken toy. He was pretty certain a body lay near the stage. From the tiny blob of color he would say it was a woman. Was it Myra? He hoped so.

Kincaid stared until his eyes watered. He knuckled them dry, swearing at himself again. He was merely putting off what he knew he had to do.

He swung down, and his knees were strangely weak. For an instant, he thought they might refuse to support him. What if she isn't dead? That treacherous, little thought stole into his mind, driving him frantic. He fought the insidious power of the thought. He wouldn't allow it to be so. She had to be dead. Nobody could have survived that wreck.

He started down the slope, taking mincing steps, digging in his heels to keep from building up momentum. If he gave way to the pull of this slope, his steps would grow longer and faster until he lost his balance. If he fell, he could roll and tumble the remainder of the descent.

He had been cold and shivering when he started down, but now he was sweating as he fought the slope.

Some fifty yards ahead of him a body lay lodged behind a stunted bush. The bush kept the man from going all the way down.

Kincaid approached cautiously. 'Coe,' he said aloud, a mean satisfaction in his voice. He couldn't see any life, but he didn't relinquish any of his caution as he closed the distance. His satisfaction grew. If Coe wasn't dead, nobody would ever give a better imitation of a corpse.

Kincaid slid the last half-dozen feet to Coe. Little cascades of pebbles and sand flowed down the slope ahead of him, lodging against Coe's body.

Kincaid studied Coe with savage intensity, not sure what he would do if Coe was still alive. Coe was hatless, and the raw, ugly gash had ripped halfway across his head. It had peeled away a good part of the scalp, and Kincaid was sure he saw the white of bone. Some of his tension eased. Nobody could survive a wound like that.

Coe lay on his back, and he had bled profusely. A curtain of blood covered his face. Kincaid hated to touch him, but he must be sure Coe was dead. Kincaid bent close and listened. He couldn't hear the slightest sound, and there was no movement in those parted lips.

Straightening abruptly almost cost him his balance. His lips twisted sardonically. That would be a hell of a note, to come this far, then ruin everything by falling and rolling down the steep slope.

He prodded Coe with the toe of his boot and saw no response. He made sure of his balance before he kicked Coe with savage intensity. The kick pulled no response from Coe except for the normal movement of his body under the impact of the boot toe.

Kincaid watched him a moment longer. He was certain Coe was dead. He went on down the slope, not letting his rising exultation make him too careless. So far, everything had gone even better than he hoped for. He remembered how he felt up there on the road, the doubt and the fear. He could discard all that now. Luck was with him. Finding Coe dead was an indication of how well things were turning out for him.

Kincaid approached the stage, a tentative step at a time, his ears alert to pick up the faintest sound, his eyes flicking constantly all around to pick up the slightest movement. He breathed faster, and his sweating had stopped. This scene was so eerily quiet.

Awe returned to him as he looked at the stage. He had never seen a vehicle more thoroughly wrecked. All it was good for now was firewood.

A man lay a dozen feet from the wreckage. Kincaid shuddered as he looked at him. There was no doubt about this one, either. Some savage force had almost torn his head off his body.

A woman, battered, and broken, was inside the stage. All he could make out about her was that she wasn't Myra.

His lips were drawn taut, and his breathing whistled shrilly. That spot of color he had seen from the road had to be Myra. He moved around the stage, his congesting throat making his breathing difficult. A woman lay before him. Kincaid knew that dress well. He had picked it out for Myra.

He stood over her, steeling himself before

he could finally look at her. His eyes moved to her face. He shook as though he was in the grip of a hard chill. Her eyes were closed in a waxen face. By the queer angle of an arm and leg, Kincaid was sure Myra had suffered broken bones.

Kincaid's breath left him in an explosive burst. He wanted to yell with his swelling triumph. He had watched the stage load this morning, counting only two passengers beside Myra. He had accounted for all the passengers and Coe. They were all dead. He almost whimpered in his relief. Myra wasn't alive to tell anybody about the quarrel between them last night. The Bannock Stage Line was all his.

His eyes widened in horror, as he saw the slight fluttering of Myra's eyelids. Shock held him in its relentless hold. Her head moved. Hearing her moan was the final blow. Myra was still alive.

For a long moment, Kincaid couldn't move, and his sluggish mind rejected any coherent thought. Myra was alive. Kincaid wanted to scream his protest at the irony of the fates. He had been so close. Now success was going to be snatched from him. Even if she didn't recover, she might live long enough to regain consciousness and talk. If her thoughts were lucid enough, she might say that she didn't want the business going to him.

She moaned again, and he thought some color was returning to her face. He wanted to rave and rant in his despair. To be this close and have the door slammed in his face— He sobbed uncontrollably and couldn't finish the thought. He wasn't going to let it turn out like this.

The pistol was half out of his coat pocket before he got hold of his thinking. A bullet wouldn't do. It would stop her from talking, but it would arouse ugly suspicions. This had to look like only an unfortunate accident.

He looked wildly about him, and his eyes picked out a fair-sized rock, laying a dozen feet from Myra. He ran to it, bent, and picked it up. It had considerable weight, for he panted and grunted under the load. He carried it back and raised it as high as he could over Myra's head. He dashed it down with all the force he could command.

He heard, or imagined he heard, the ugly crunching sound. He jerked his eyes away before they fully took in the scene. He would not let them register this horror.

He turned away, his breathing clogging in

his throat. His heart pounded so that it dizzied him. One thing was certain. Myra would never talk to anybody.

He turned his back on the scene, waiting for a degree of calmness to ease his breathing and clear his eyes. It was all done now, he thought dully. Maybe later, the former triumphant feeling would return. Now, he was too emotionally spent.

The eerie silence was growing until he wanted to scream against its pressures. He had to get out of here as fast as he could. He climbed the slope, clawing his way upward. Several times he thought he was going to lose his balance and fall, but he forced himself on.

He passed Coe's body, and it hadn't moved. Kincaid was wringing wet with sweat when he finally reached the top.

He had to lean against his horse for support before he found enough strength to mount. He glanced at the scene below him before he turned the horse. The trembling was subsiding, and he could think clearly again. Nobody down there would be able to speak about this unfortunate accident.

CHAPTER SEVEN

Coe thought he might be conscious, but he couldn't be sure. He seemed to be floating in a black void, and he couldn't hear a sound. Was this death? He pondered over the perplexing problem. It was odd if it was, for he could think; not lucidly, but in little grabs for fragments of ideas. He decided he didn't like it, for it was too dark and lonely.

A shattering pain ripped through his head, jerking him back to reality. For a moment, there was no organized thought, only the enduring of that shattering pain. He thought he opened his mouth and howled against the agony, but, if he did, he couldn't hear himself. He was sure his eyes were open, but he couldn't see. Oh God, he was deaf and blind.

The pain must have lasted for at least an eternity before it eased off. Did he hear the sound of crying near him? But that couldn't be. He had just convinced himself he was deaf. But the crying went on, little mewling cries sounding like a badly hurt animal.

He tried to call out to the maker of that sound. Whoever it was wouldn't answer him. That angered him, and he wanted to swear at the unfeeling bastard. But the crying had stopped, and he thought about it. Nobody near him was crying; that sound was coming from him.

The discovery shocked him. He must be in bad shape to give way to that kind of weakness. But the discovery did another thing for him. It sharpened his thinking and stripped some of the dross from it. He wasn't deaf, or he wouldn't have heard that crying. He didn't know where he was, but wherever it was, he was cold, and he hurt. He forced his thoughts into new harsh discipline. If he wasn't deaf, then maybe he wasn't blind, either.

He forced his eyes open, and felt the stir of excitement race along his pulses. He couldn't see plainly, and everything was fuzzy, but he could see light. He tried to peer harder through the curtain that was impeding his vision. He blinked to clear his eyes and his eyelids moved sluggishly. They felt gummy as though something sticky had been poured into them, and he had to rest before he could think about that.

My God, he was so tired. Just thinking was

an effort. But he kept blinking his eyes and his vision kept clearing, but the stickiness was still there.

He lay there, thinking of the pain that had pounded at him a moment ago. Its fierce sharpness was gone, but the dull hammering in his head remained. He was almost sure he wasn't dead, for he was aware of too many sensations.

Then how had he gotten here, and where was he? Had he been hurt? He could answer the last question with a definite Yes. Trying to answer all those questions was too much effort for his weary mind.

Enough strength filtered back to him so that he could raise a hand to his eyes. He was right about his first impression; they felt sticky, but whatever it was, he could remove flakes of it. Each time, he cleared a little of it away, his vision improved. He stared dully at a small flake in his fingers. For an instant, he couldn't make out what it was. Originally, it could have been a bright red, but now it was turning into a drab brown. The answer he was seeking slammed into him with the force of an actual blow. That was blood, and it had to be his own. He struggled for an answer to this new and perplexing question. He felt over his face, feeling the same drying flakes.

He must have bled a lot. But how had it happened; who was responsible for it? He knew only one thing for certain – he must have been here for quite a while for the blood to be this dry.

His fingers rose and touched the gash in his head. He winced and jerked his fingers away. Just touching that raw wound sent off a new onslaught of relentless pain. It shook him like a terrier shakes a rat. He gritted his teeth to keep from howling.

He waited in dull resignation for the pain to lessen before he could try again to reason his way through this. How in the hell had he gotten into this mess?

The answer hit him all at once, as bright and terrifying as a near bolt of lightning. He remembered the rise of the driver's seat, the inexorable pressure that pushed him into space. He remembered jumping, and after that there was nothing.

Oh my God, he groaned. The stage. He had driven too close to the road's edge, and the stage had gone over. There were passengers on that stage, and, worst of all, Myra had been riding with him.

His sobbing clogged in his throat, hampering his breathing. How bad was the wreck; how many were hurt?

He knew what he had to do, yet he still lay here, refusing to face reality. Some inner voice flogged him mercilessly. You caused it, the voice accused. You thought you were so damned sharp. Those drinks last night, or those he drank this morning had made him careless. His normal reflexes had been dulled. If it hadn't been for those drinks, he wouldn't have made that stupid blunder.

Are you going down there and see what happened – the voice flogged him – or are you going to run away?

He wished to God he could. He would have given anything to avoid looking at the damage he caused. He couldn't live with that inner flogging now. If he didn't go down there, it would only grow worse.

He forced himself to stand, biting his lower lip to keep from yelling. He reeled and was sure he would fall again. Only strength of will held him erect. He forced himself to look down the slope. His vision was much better, but he still couldn't make out the stage plainly. He was sure it was battered beyond recognition, and he groaned again.

He went down the slope with small, careful steps, knowing that if he tried to hurry he would certainly fall. Maybe the pounding in his head was an asset. It kept forcing him on.

Halfway down the slope, he passed the bodies of two of the horses. He stared at the broken and battered bodies. Dandy and Blister had been good horses.

Coe shuddered and turned his face away. If the horses hadn't survived, how could he hope that the passengers had?

He wasn't sure how he finished that terrible descent to the bottom. He was light-headed and unsure of every step when he finally approached the stage. He stared at the wreckage with lackluster eyes, but it registered with him. He had seen other stages that had plunged from the road and rolled over and over before they came to rest, but never anything like this.

Coe made himself look at the body of the man, lying a few yards from the battered vehicle. A terrible force had almost decapitated him, and the uneasy motion of Coe's stomach accelerated and began to take on a rolling, heaving swell. Oh God, he thought over and over. There had been others in the stage, but for the moment, Coe was unable to face them.

He clenched his jaws, trying to stop that swell in his stomach. He put a final look on the body, trying to keep out the thought that forced itself into his mind. This man had definitely been killed by Coe's bad driving. And his bad driving came out of a bottle.

He wanted to drop to his knees and scream his innocence. Coe didn't want this at all; he hadn't intended a few, harmless drinks to end in tragedy.

He forced himself to see what remained in the stage. A woman's body was in the interior. He didn't have to touch her to know she hadn't survived, either.

He still hadn't found Myra, and a faint hope flickered in him. That was foolish wishing. If these two passengers hadn't lived through his, how could he expect Myra to?

He walked around the stage, and Myra lay before him. The fascination of horror held his eyes on her for a long, agonized moment. Her crushed head was unrecognizable, but he knew what she had worn today. This poor, sorry thing was Myra.

The nausea rose in an unstoppable wave, and he vomited. The wracking spasm finally ended in dry retchings that left him limp and unsteady.

His head and eyes finally cleared, and he looked at her in final, bitter self-rebuke. 'Oh God, Myra,' he whispered, 'I'm sorry. So damned sorry.'

He turned blindly away to commence the torturous ascent to the road. He had to tell somebody about this.

A dozen times he thought he would never make it. He clawed his way up the last remaining hundred yards, on hands and knees. He staggered to the middle of the road before he fell. There wasn't even enough strength left for him to get back to his feet. He tried until he sobbed with frustration, but his weakened arms refused to lift his body more than a few inches from the ground.

He fought to keep his consciousness from slipping away. Sooner or later, somebody had to come along; he had to be able to tell them what had happened.

A great wall of blackness was encroaching upon him. This was a fight he couldn't win. All of his remaining strength was behind his yell, then he knew nothing else.

CHAPTER EIGHT

Coe stared blankly about him as consciousness slowly returned. He remembered falling, he remembered yelling, or trying to, but
this wasn't the same place. He was in a
small, bleak room, and he tried to puzzle
how that could be.

Coe tried to lift his head, and a hand
gently pushed him back onto the table.

'Easy, Coe,' a voice said, 'I'm not through
with you yet.'

The voice had a familiar ring, but Coe
couldn't place it.

'Who is it?' he asked weakly. Somebody
was behind him, and he felt their fingers
working on his head. Each touch sent a new
wave of pure fire through his skull. What the
hell were they doing to him?

'Are you trying to kill me?' he demanded.

The dry chuckle held grim humor. 'I don't
have to, Coe. You damned near did that
yourself.'

The chuckle and remark placed the voice
for Coe. Nobody but Jason Biddle sounded

94

like that. Coe tried to turn his head as he said, 'How did I get here?'

Strong fingers held his head immobile. 'Damn it, I told you I'm not through. Will you hold still?'

Something moist was splashed into the wound in Coe's head, and it relit that hell-fire. This time, it was surely going to rip off his head.

His eyes filled with water, and he couldn't talk. When he finally got his voice back, he gasped, 'A meat ax would do it quicker.'

Again, there was that dry, amused chuckle. 'I couldn't equal the job you tried to do,' Biddle said. 'That's a nasty gash, Coe. Sure, it hurts. But do you want it to get infected? Just another minute or two, and I'll be through.'

Biddle hummed tunelessly as he worked. The pressure of his fingers kept Coe wincing. He moved into Coe's view, his head cocked. He was a small man, beginning to bend under the onslaught of age, but he was still spry, and his eyes were kind.

'You're going to look like hell for a couple of weeks,' he observed. 'I had to shave your head to get at that wound. I guess you feel as bad as you look,' he said sympathetically.

Coe sat up, and that awful pain grabbed

him again. The color drained from his face.

'I was just going to tell you to take it easy,' Biddle said reprovingly. 'But you moved too fast. I guess you found that out.' He shook his head, wonder showing on his face. 'I don't know how you came through this, Coe. I guess you can thank your hard head. Do you want to take a look at yourself?'

Coe nodded mutely. He swung his feet to the floor. When he tried to stand, his legs felt as limber as string. The room swayed and dipped, and he put a hand on the table to steady himself. 'My God, I'm weak.'

Biddle snorted. 'What did you expect? Lean on me and take it slow.'

Coe needed the advice and the help. Without Biddle he couldn't have made it to the mirror.

He stared at his reflection. Biddle had shaved half of his head, then covered the area with a bandage. That battered head was causing Coe most of his trouble, but his face looked far worse. He had two heavy bruises on it and several scraped raw patches. He rubbed finger tips over the raw area on his chin and winced.

Biddle caught both the wince and expression. 'Couldn't do much about those skinned places,' he said cheerfully. 'For a

96

while they're going to give you hell whe
you try to shave. My advice is to let you
beard grow until your face is healed.'

That stunned, dazed look in Coe's eyes
worried Biddle. Was Coe in shock? A
moment ago, Biddle hadn't thought so.
Now, he wasn't so sure. He spoke rapidly to
take Coe's fixed attention from his reflection. 'I want you to come in, in a day or two,
Coe. That bandage will have to be changed.'

He frowned as Coe's expression didn't
change. Coe's face was a mask of tragedy.
Was Coe grieving that much over his
wounds? Biddle snorted at the ridiculous
idea. Only one of those wounds was serious,
and that would heal with care and time.
There was no reason why it shouldn't. Coe
was as healthy as an ox. But something had
a relentless grip on Coe's mind.

'Didn't you hear me, Coe?' Biddle snapped. Coe looked at him with dull eyes, and
Biddle's ire rose. It was time to snap the
whip and get Coe out of this mood.

'Goddamn it, Coe. Stop feeling sorry for
yourself. You're lucky to be alive. Don't you
realize you could be dead right now?'

'I wish I was,' Coe said lifelessly.

That shocked Biddle. His jaw sagged, and
he spit and spluttered before he could talk.

'That's a hell of a thing to say,' he said severely. 'Why dammit. I think you should be grateful. After what happened–'

Coe wearily waved him quiet. 'It doesn't matter,' he said indifferently. 'How did I get here?' He didn't want to speak of what he had seen at the bottom of that hill, at least not yet.

'Old Wilkie Holt found you in the middle of the road,' Biddle said sternly. 'He was driving into town. He had a hell of a struggle getting you into the wagon. You were out of your head. Wilkie said you raved and cussed all the way here.'

Coe's eyes were fixed on Biddle with an odd intensity. 'What did I say?'

'Just the usual crazy stuff a man in your shape would babble,' Biddle said uncomfortably. He shifted his eyes from Coe's face. He would never look at more spiritual distress in a man's eyes.

'Did I mention the stage wreck?' Coe asked in a low voice.

'Over and over,' Biddle replied. 'Wilkie saw it from the road. He didn't go down.'

'There was no need,' Coe said dully. 'Myra and the others. I killed them, Jason.'

Biddle's eyes were round with horror. 'Myra was on that stage?' At Coe's somber

98

nod, Biddle cried, 'Oh, goddamn it. Is she–'
He didn't finish. Myra was a well-liked
person.

'She's dead,' Coe said harshly. 'I went
down to see. All the passengers were dead.'
His voice rose higher and higher. 'I was the
only one who got out of it alive. He tried to
laugh and failed. 'You explain that to me.'

Biddle thought he had the answer to the
sickness in Coe's eyes. He was well aware of
what Coe thought of Brad and Myra Bannock.

'Here now,' he said brusquely, 'you can't
be blaming yourself, Coe. That's a bad
stretch of road. The stage just went over the
edge. That's all. My God, man, you're not
the first driver who's had an accident. You
won't be the last.'

Coe sucked in a deep breath. That didn't
help, nor did Biddle's attempt to console
him. If anything, Coe's eyes looked more
frantic than ever.

'Where's my coat?' he demanded.

Biddle's eyes were worried as he pointed
to the sheepskin hanging from a nail on the
wall. He couldn't help but wonder if Coe
had fully regained his senses.

Coe turned toward his coat. Biddle sprang
forward to help him. Coe waved him away

with a savage gesture.

Coe reached the coat and ran his hand into a pocket. It was amazing, but even after his fall down the slope, the bottle was still intact. He pulled out the bottle and held it up.

Both of them were so intent on what Coe was doing that neither of them saw nor heard Sheriff Jude Kirby open the door and enter. Kirby opened his mouth to speak, but something in the strained attitudes of Biddle and Coe arrested his words. His eyes narrowed. He had learned long ago that observance was almost as informative as direct questions.

He closed the door softly and leaned against it. Kirby was a small, bandy-legged man, with cold gray eyes in a rugged face. He had lived long enough so that nothing anybody did surprised him.

'Do you see this?' Coe demanded. 'If you're searching for whys, this is the principle one. Don't try to forgive me, Jason.' His voice lowered to a whisper. 'I can't.'

'What are you talking about?' Biddle managed to say.

'If you're looking for the cause of the accident, this is it.'

Biddle's face was twisted with concern. 'Now wait a minute, Coe,' he started.

'No,' Coe said savagely. 'It wasn't a simple accident. I just drove over the edge.'

Biddle's mouth opened in shock. 'Aw, Coe. You don't know what you're saying.'

'The hell I don't,' Coe shouted. 'I was drunk last night. I had three more drinks this morning.' He glared at Biddle. 'You must have smelled the liquor on me while you were patching me up.'

Biddle wanted to shake his head but held the gesture. This was no time to be lying to Coe. 'Aw, Coe,' he said miserably, 'you're building something up out of all proportion.'

'Don't try to be making excuses for me, Jason,' Coe snapped. 'I never drove over the edge before, did I? I killed Myra and the others.' For a moment the hard mask of his face broke, and the tormented spirit showed through. Then the cracks healed, and the frozen expression was back in place.

'I know what happened, and I know the cause of it,' Coe said savagely. He hurled the bottle at the far wall. The sound of shattering glass was loud in the still room. The whiskey stained the wall, then slowly ran down in little rivulets.

Biddle still tried to reason with Coe. 'Being drunk last night doesn't mean you were drunk this morning. Three drinks this morning wouldn't have done that.'

Kirby thought it was time to step in. 'Maybe it did,' he said dryly and moved forward.

Both heads jerked toward him. 'Now just a minute, Jude,' Biddle said hotly. 'Don't go jumping to any conclusion from a few words you heard. Coe doesn't know what he's saying this morning.'

'I think he does,' Kirby drawled. His eyes weren't too friendly as he looked at Coe. Coe's drinking had caused him trouble on several occasions.

Biddle's face was flushed with anger. 'You're trying to make it worse than it is.'

'I talked to Wilkie a few minutes ago. He told me about picking up Coe. He said I'd find him here.' Kirby's face was relentless. 'Three people are dead. I can't make it much worse than that, can I? I'm not accusing Coe of deliberate murder. But goddamn it, somebody's responsible for all this.'

Biddle opened his mouth. Coe shook his head wearily, cutting off Biddle's words. He looked weak and utterly spent.

'Jude's right,' Coe said in a voice barely audible.

Biddle wasn't through. 'Damn it, Jude. You can't lock him up like some common criminal.'

'I can until I do some more looking into this,' Kirby snapped. He added with emphasis, 'Myra was a popular woman. The town's going to be pretty upset over her death.'

'You always were thickheaded, Jude,' Biddle said scornfully. 'You tell me how you're going to do yourself any good making this out to be anything but an accident.'

Biddle's words must have bitten deep, for Kirby flushed and his eyes flared. He checked himself and said reasonably enough, 'All I said was that this needs looking into. I don't stand over you and tell you how to do your work, do I?'

That was an honest enough question, but it made Biddle's face burn. He stared at the floor and didn't speak.

'You ready to go, Coe?' Kirby asked.

'Yes,' Coe replied woodenly.

CHAPTER NINE

Coe guessed Kirby was taking him to jail, and he didn't much care. The jail was three blocks away, and he wasn't sure he could make it. He was so damned weak. His knees threatened to buckle with each step. He walked with his eyes on the ground, grateful that Kirby hadn't said anything since they left Biddle's office. He was well aware of how Kirby felt about him.

'You keep your mouth shut,' Kirby said suddenly.

Coe's expression was puzzled as he glanced at Kirby. What had brought that on? Kirby stared straight ahead, and Coe turned his head to see what drew Kirby's attention. Five men were on the street corner ahead. Coe's heart picked up a rapid, uneven beat. He knew all five well, and he didn't need to be any closer to their angry faces to know they didn't mean him any good.

'Just keep moving,' Kirby said in a low voice. 'I'll do all the talking. You keep your mouth shut. You hear me?'

Kirby didn't have to warn Coe of that. Coe didn't want to talk to anybody, particularly these five men.

Jett Kincaid stood a little before the other four. The others were Landler, Inder, Westhoff, and Rickles. Landler and Inder were drivers for the stage line, Westhoff worked in the office, and Rickles was the company's blacksmith. Kincaid's mouth worked convulsively, and he looked as though he was in the grip of grief and rage. The other four glowered at Kirby and Coe. Coe was sure all their hostility was directed solely at him.

'Here comes the damned woman killer,' Rickles shouted. He was a brawny man with shoulders and arms developed by his years of work at an anvil.

Coe winced more at the words Rickles shouted, than at any thought of those powerful hands taking hold of him. He considered Rickles a friend as he did all the others, except Kincaid. He had spent many an evening drinking and laughing with these men. He could see no trace of those memories on any of their faces. Oh God, he thought frantically. He would give anything if he could turn and run.

'Keep on moving,' Kirby said softly.

The five men fanned out, blocking the

way. They know about Myra, Coe thought dully. They know what happened. He guessed the whole town knew by now.

'You killed my wife,' Kincaid screamed. 'Goddamn you–' A sob broke off the remainder of his words. His eyes were crazed in a maniac's face.

The other four growled in response. They sounded like a pack of animals ready to rend and tear.

Coe held out a pleading hand. 'You know I didn't want that, Jett. It was an accident. All of you knew what I thought of Myra.'

Only Kincaid didn't curse Coe. The four used every foul word they knew. Kincaid just stared at him with those wild eyes.

'That's doing no good,' Kirby growled. 'Go ahead, Coe.'

Nobody moved out of Coe's path.

'Maybe it wasn't an accident.' Kincaid's voice rose higher and higher. 'Maybe Myra told you she was going to fire you. We talked about it last night, and she agreed it had to be done.' He was screaming now. 'I think she told you this morning, and you wanted to get even.'

Coe was appalled. 'You think I deliberately drove over the edge, Jett? I went over, too.'

That didn't ease Kincaid's crazed expression. 'I know you were drunk last night. Maybe you were still drunk this morning. When she fired you, I think that was the last straw. Your head was so filled with liquor that you wanted to do anything that occurred to you. You deliberately drove over the edge.'

Coe stubbornly shook his head. 'I wasn't drunk this morning, Jett. Myra didn't fire me. I had no reason.'

He glanced helplessly from face to face, seeking a little understanding from any of them. Kirby looked as antagonistic as the others, perhaps not so vindictive, but still unforgiving.

'This ain't solving anything,' Kirby said sharply. 'I'm looking into it. Keep out of it.'

'I know what you'll do with him,' Kincaid yelled. 'Lock him up for a few days and feed him at taxpayers' expense before you turn him loose. Will that bring her back?'

The four were in complete accord with Kincaid, and four heads bobbed in agreement.

'Hell no,' Landler said.

'We can take him off of your hands, Jude,' Rickles said. 'Just say the word, Jett.'

Some of the wildness faded from Kincaid's face. Now, it was only ugly and mean. He breathed hard and said slowly, 'I demand immediate punishment. Maybe we ought to smash his head like Myra's was.'

All of them surged forward as if by some simultaneous signal.

'Hold it,' Kirby roared. 'Hold it.'

The threat of physical violence wasn't what sickened Coe. It was the monstrously twisted facts in every one of their minds. All of them knew what Myra meant to him.

'Listen–' he started.

His plea didn't stop them any more than Kirby's order. They came at him from all sides. Kirby tried to hold them back, but he couldn't handle all of them at once. 'Get back,' he kept yelling.

The faces coming at Coe were ravaged masks of hate. Still, Coe made no effort to defend himself. He was chalky white, and his lips were a thin, bloodless line. He felt no censure for their actions. How could he blame them when he knew how much of the blame was his?

In their eagerness to get at him, they impeded each other, and that momentarily saved Coe. He didn't see the first fist fly, but he felt it. It bounced off his ear, and he wanted to yell under the flooding hurt. The blow revitalized the former pain, adding a new degree of intensity. He thought his head was going to burst under the throbbing. Another fist grazed a cheekbone, and that started a new pain, different from the first but fully as piercing.

All Coe did was lower his head and throw up both arms to protect his face. Blows rained in on him from all sides, making his head reel, and drawing the strength out of his legs. Still, he didn't go down.

Kirby raved like a madman as he struggled against Coe's attackers. Every time he threw one of them aside, another came at Coe from another angle. Kirby struck out with fists and kicked out with boots, and still he couldn't deter them.

'Oh, you bastards,' Kirby swore. 'All right, if that's the way you want it.' He jerked out his gun and crashed the barrel against Inder's head. A hollow groan escaped Inder, and his face went slack. His eyes rolled up into his head, and he fell as though his legs were kicked out from under him. He hit the ground and lay there, looking like a bundle of discarded clothing.

Kirby struck out at Westhoff. Westhoff jerked his head aside, trying to escape the full brunt of the blow. He saved his head, but the barrel smashed across his shoulder. He howled in animal pain and sagged against a building wall, one hand holding the throbbing shoulder.

Landler and Rickles realized what Kirby was doing, and his determination got through to them. They backed away from Coe, their faces apprehensive.

'By God, Kirby,' Landler said in disbelief. 'You're protecting him.'

Kirby was worked up to an insane pitch. 'If you haven't learned enough, try it again.' He gestured with the pistol. 'The next time I use this, it'll stop you for good.' His full attention was on the two, and he took his eyes off of Kincaid.

It gave Kincaid the opportunity he sought. He ran at Coe, smashing at him with both fists. Coe had a hazy impression of a slobbering, maniacal face. Kincaid yelled something but Coe couldn't make out the words.

The blows rocked him, but he didn't feel any additional pain. But they were taking their toll, for his strength was ebbing from him. He sank to the ground. Kincaid kicked him again, and Coe gasped from the impact.

'I'll kill you,' Kincaid raved. 'I'll kick you to death.'

He probably would have, for Coe was helpless to stop him. Kirby did that. He whirled and bounded at Kincaid, ramming his shoulder into Kincaid's back. He knocked Kincaid away from Coe, sending him into a series of staggering, broken steps. Kincaid crashed into a wall and fell. He turned a stupefied face toward Kirby.

Kirby was livid with fury. 'Try some more of that, Jett. I want you to.'

Kincaid looked at those merciless eyes, and his insane rage filtered away. 'I had every right,' he said sullenly.

'Lean on that right and see how far it gets you,' Kirby snapped.

Kincaid couldn't meet Kirby's eyes, and he looked at the ground. 'This isn't over yet,' he muttered.

'Your part in it is,' Kirby said coldly. He swung his head and looked at Inder and Rickles. 'You two got a different opinion?'

They wouldn't look at him. That was answer enough.

Kirby came back to Coe. 'Can you make it?' he asked gruffly.

Coe shook his head and blinked his eyes several times to clear them. 'I can make it,' he said weakly.

Without Kirby's assistance, he couldn't have. Coe needed the support of Kirby's shoulder, for his legs insisted upon buckling on him. He took a step and despite his clenched teeth, a groan forced its way through them.

'What is it?' Kirby demanded, his eyes darkening. Fury still boiled within him. He didn't give a damn who it was. Nobody manhandled a prisoner of his like this.

'Feels like Kincaid kicked in a rib,' Coe replied.

'Your face is bleeding, too,' Kirby said. 'As soon as I get you to jail, I'll get Doc Biddle. You need some attention.'

'I'll be all right,' Coe said stoically.

'From now on, things will be run my way,' Kirby snapped. He was still furious at the intervention of Kincaid and the others. 'By God, they were out of their minds. I should have busted some heads at the beginning. I wish to God they'd try that again.'

Coe managed a wan grin. 'Not to me, Jude. I've had more than enough to last me for a long time.' He looked at Kirby's scowling face and said earnestly, 'I can't blame them too much, Jude. Myra meant a lot to all of them.'

'You're too damned forgiving,' Kirby said sourly.

Each step was a torture to Coe, but he endured them. Kirby's jail must be a good ten miles away.

CHAPTER TEN

Kirby hesitated before he left Coe's cell. Coe was stretched out on his back. If he stayed in that position, it eased the stabbing pain in his ribs. It also helped his aching head. Kirby had given him a pan of water and a cloth so he could wash the blood off his battered face. One day like this in a lifetime was all Coe wanted.

'Sure I can't do anything else for you?'

Coe shook his head but didn't open his eyes. All he wanted was to lie here and die quietly.

'I could pour you a drink, Coe,' Kirby suggested.

Coe's reaction to that was violent and unwise. He sat up too quickly, and it set all the devils of pain twisting and pulling at him. He glared at Kirby and waited for the catch in his breathing to ease. 'Damn you,' he said huskily. 'If that's your idea of a joke, it's a damn poor one. I don't want a drink.'

Kirby grimaced in self-reproval. Coe sure sounded as though he meant that. Hard drinking had gotten Coe into this mess. At the moment, another drink was the farthest thing from Coe's mind.

'Sure, Coe,' Kirby said in apology. 'I'll be back as quick as I can.'

Kirby's face was thoughtful as he stepped out onto the street. Most of Coe's suffering didn't seem to come from his physical hurts. Kirby had noted the spiritual anguish that shadowed Coe's eyes. The physical suffering was superficial, for time would take care of it. Kirby wasn't so sure about the spiritual aspect.

There was no doubt that Coe hadn't wanted a drink now. How long would that last? Kirby hadn't the slightest idea. But Coe's haunted eyes showed how severe a shock he had suffered. Kincaid and the others might not believe Coe when he spoke of how much Myra meant to him. Kirby did. Hell, no one could look at Coe and listen to him when he spoke about Myra and not fail to see how sincere he was. Coe would carry the spiritual scars of this morning the rest of his life.

Kirby spat at the walk, his face reflective. A man sure built his own particular brand of hell.

A wagon was drawn up before Bradshaw's

undertaking establishment, and a dozen people were gathered around it. Kirby had an inkling of what the attraction was before he spoke to anybody.

He touched Merl Maynes on the shoulder. 'What's going on here?'

Maynes was a pudgy man with a soft, doughy face. He ran a restaurant, and by the fat building up on him, he liked his own cooking too well.

Maynes looked angrily at Kirby. 'They just brought Myra and the others in. It's a goddamned shame.'

'What's a shame?' Kirby asked testily. He was afraid he knew the answer. He had seen a similar reaction just a short while ago.

Maynes's indignation built. 'It's a damned shame to let a drunk like Coe Dahmer kill a woman like Myra Kincaid.'

Kirby stared coldly at him. Maynes was working himself into a high pitch. Kirby felt a touch of alarm. When a little, inoffensive man like Maynes displayed this much outrage, it spoke of how rampant emotion over town was growing. It wouldn't take much for that emotion to break into violent action. Kirby had seen enough of that in Kincaid and the others.

'What about the others in the stage?'

115

Kirby snapped. 'Don't they matter?'

'I never said that,' Maynes flared.

'You didn't know them as well. Is that it?'

Maynes flushed. 'Don't you be trying to put words in my mouth. Sure, I'm sorry for them. It's just that I knew Myra so well. She was a fine woman. To die like that–' He shook his head. 'It's just a damned shame.'

Their talk drew the attention of the other people, and they crowded closer around Maynes and Kirby.

'Nobody's denying that,' Kirby said wearily.

'Something should be done about it,' Maynes insisted.

Kirby felt that icy touch of alarm again. 'You got a solution for it, Maynes?' Expressing sorrow was one thing; to bolster it with action was an entirely different matter.

'I say that drunken bum should be punished,' Maynes said shrilly. Heads all around him bobbed in vicious agreement.

Kirby's temper broke. People might profess to abhor violence, but they gravitated to it, particularly when a group, feeling the same way, was gathered. There was no telling to what lengths raw passion would drive them.

'Listen, all of you,' Kirby snapped. 'You keep your noses out of this. It's happened. Nothing can change that. I won't have you standing around, encouraging each other to some crazy action. The law will do whatever can be done about this. Remember that.'

Kirby sighed. By the sullen expressions on their faces, he knew he hadn't reached them. What had been displayed by Kincaid and his people, and now this bunch, wasn't thinking; it was raw, animal-like passion that demanded something to get their claws into. If this feeling spread all over town, Kirby didn't know what he might have on his hands. It could spread, he thought gloomily. Too easily.

He searched for something else to say that would carry conviction and only came up with, 'You remember what I said.'

Kirby glared about at each face, and eyes shifted away from his. He knew he hadn't touched them yet. He felt a rising despondency. Too often, a feeling like this had to be met with a physical clubbing. Kirby hated the thought of having to face another situation like the encounter with Kincaid. He guessed his age was beginning to show.

He looked back after a dozen strides. Those people had their heads together again. While he couldn't hear what they were saying, he knew they were verbally tearing him apart.

'The damned hard heads,' he muttered.

Bill Crawford hurried down the street

toward Bradshaw's, and Kirby stopped him.

'What's going on down there?' Crawford asked. 'I saw the bunch of people there and thought I'd better look into it.'

He shifted his weight, and his face contorted.

That gimpy leg must be giving him hell today, Kirby thought. He wondered if Crawford knew about Coe. That could be the reason for his hurry.

He spoke before Crawford could. 'Bill, they just brought Myra and the other stage passengers into Bradshaw's. All of them are dead.'

'Oh God, no.' Crawford was shaking visibly. 'I heard some vague talk about an accident. That wasn't the stage Coe was driving, was it?' His tone pleaded for Kirby to deny it.

'It was,' Kirby replied. 'Coe was the only one who got out alive. He was hurt, but he'll be all right.'

Crawford paled. It made his cheekbones stand out sharply. 'It was an accident,' he said, his voice shaky. 'The law of averages says that a driver who's been at it as long as Coe is bound to have one sooner or later.'

'Unless there's another factor,' Kirby said softly.

Crawford flared. 'What the hell are you trying to say, Jude? That Coe caused that accident?'

Kirby's eyes were troubled. 'Not consciously, Bill. Coe was drunk last night, wasn't he?'

Crawford wanted badly to deny that. It was in his eyes that refused to hold on Kirby's face. He caved in all at once. 'All right,' he said and sighed. It wouldn't do any good to lie about this. Everybody in Brown's saloon knew how hard Coe had drunk last night. 'But he didn't start that fight with Kincaid. Kincaid took the first swing at Coe. Coe had to knock him down, didn't he?'

Kirby's eyes were hard and alert. 'Ah,' he murmured, 'that's news to me.' Kincaid wasn't a forgiving man. How much of last night's fight was in Kincaid's actions when he jumped Coe a little while ago? It was an interesting question. Kirby filed it away for future reference.

'He wasn't drunk this morning,' Crawford said stubbornly. 'Damn it, Jude, don't you think I'd know? I woke him up and talked to him. He was all right.'

'Maybe he was when he went out,' Kirby said. 'But I heard him tell Doc Biddle he had three drinks this morning. What did that do?

119

Was it enough to rekindle last night's fire?'

'You're accusing him of being drunk, aren't you?' Crawford asked miserably.

Kirby was sorry for Crawford. 'I'm not accusing him of anything yet,' he said flatly. 'But Coe thinks he was responsible.' At the denial forming in Crawford's face, he said heatedly. 'I've seen and talked to him. I'll never look at a sicker man, and it wasn't from his injuries.'

All of Crawford's resistance collapsed. 'My God, Jude, you know what Myra meant to Coe. He wouldn't do anything to harm her.'

'Not willingly,' Kirby conceded. 'But the accident happened. I've got to find out if anybody's legally responsible.'

A little color was stealing back in Crawford's face. 'That means Coe, doesn't it?'

Kirby nodded gravely.

'Where is he, Jude? I'd like to see him.'

'I've got him locked up for his own good, Bill. Kincaid and four of his help jumped us on the way to the jail. They knocked Coe around a little before I could stop them.' He debated upon telling Crawford a second group felt the same way about Coe. He guessed it was best Crawford knew every aspect of this. He jerked his head in the direction of the people still standing before

Bradshaw's. 'They feel the same way. Myra was more popular than I realized. People are working themselves up into an ugly rage. I'm afraid it'll spread all over town. You get enough people thinking the wrong way, and God only knows what they'll try to do.'

A faint film of sweat broke out on Crawford's forehead. 'Jude, you don't think they'd try to take the law into their own hands?'

'Kincaid did,' Kirby said flatly.

'Oh Jesus,' Crawford moaned faintly.

He started to move, and Kirby said, 'The best thing you can do for Coe right now is to get Biddle. Coe needs some attention. I was going after him, but if you go, it'll let me get back to the jail. Until the town simmers down, I'll feel a lot better if I stick around close.'

That brought the paleness back into Crawford's face. 'I'll get Biddle,' Crawford said fiercely. 'You get back there and keep an eye on Coe.'

Kirby turned and lengthened his stride toward the jail. He looked back over his shoulder after a dozen paces. Crawford still stood there. He looked as though he was held in the cruel grip of shock.

Kirby gestured impatiently at him. Standing there wasn't going to do Coe any good.

CHAPTER ELEVEN

Biddle finished his examination of Coe, the scowl growing on his face. 'You've got a broken rib, Coe. All I can do is to bandage it tight. You'll be taking it easy for the next few days.' He patched up Coe's face and was swearing steadily before he was through.

'Damn it, Jude,' he said, 'from the looks of Coe, I'd say you've got the wrong man locked up.'

'If you mean Jett, you've got it wrong,' Coe said earnestly. 'Losing Myra just drove him crazy.'

'I guess you'd forgive him if he pulled out a gun and blasted you,' Biddle said testily.

'I couldn't blame him for that, either,' Coe muttered.

'I give up on you,' Biddle said in exasperation. He turned and leveled an accusing finger at Kirby. 'This could happen again. You'd better keep a close eye on him.'

'You know I will,' Kirby replied. He walked to the cell door with Biddle and looked questioningly at Crawford who hadn't moved.

'Jude, I want to stay and talk to Coe.' His eyes and tone had a pleading quality.

'I don't see why not,' Kirby said gruffly.

Crawford waited until the echoes of Biddle's and Kirby's footsteps faded.

He sat down beside Coe on the cot, his face stern. 'You tell me everything you know about this.'

Coe helplessly held out his hands. 'There's nothing to tell you, Bill. I just drove over the edge. I didn't think I was drunk,' he said mournfully. 'But maybe I was.'

'You know that better than anybody else,' Crawford snapped. 'I know you weren't drunk when you left the house. Did you drink before you picked up those reins?'

Coe's hands dangled between his knees, and he stared at them instead of at Crawford. 'I had a pint bottle hidden in the house, Bill.' His voice was barely audible. 'I took it with me. I took three drinks out of it. No more.'

'Jesus Christ,' Crawford whispered. So Kirby hadn't been wrong at all.

Coe's face begged Crawford to understand. 'The wind was cutting through me. I didn't think those drinks would make any difference. But I guess they did.' That spiritual sickness had returned to his eyes. 'I drove over the edge. Never thought it would ever happen to me.'

Crawford wanted to swear at him. He wanted to recall for Coe all the ignored advice, but held his tongue. If he tore into Coe now, it would be like kicking a man when he was down. But, oh damn, if Coe had only listened to him, all of this could have been avoided.

Crawford took a deep breath and tried to calm his jangling nerves. 'Coe, what's Kirby going to do?'

Coe shrugged in complete indifference. 'I've earned whatever he does. Bill–' His voice faded.

Crawford waited a long moment, then said gently, 'Yes, Coe?'

'Why didn't I ever listen to you?'

Crawford wearily shook his head. Coe was going through the worst punishment a man would ever know: self-judgment. With each mental flogging, his spirit would shrivel a little more.

'That's all done, Coe. It can't be changed.'

'I can change one thing,' Coe said fiercely. 'I can be damned sure that nothing like this ever happens to me again.' Again, Crawford waited out Coe's long pause. 'I'll never touch another bottle. Just looking at one will remind me of what it caused.'

Crawford hoped to God Coe meant that. But he wouldn't bank on it too strongly. From now on, each day Coe faced would only increase the vicious grinding. He sighed inwardly for Coe. Coe had just picked the hardest road a man would ever know: the road of atonement. It was a far more treacherous road than Coe had ever traveled, and he could stumble off it at any moment. Coe had to learn to live with himself. Crawford didn't envy him. Many a man hadn't been able to meet that kind of pressure without buckling.

He looked at Coe with distress-filled eyes. This wasn't the man he had known. Crawford remembered the ready laughter, the happy-go-lucky way of living. At the moment, Crawford didn't like the change, for he looked at only a hollow husk of what had been.

'I hope you meant that, Coe,' he said quietly. 'Can I do anything for you?'

Coe stared at the floor again. He shook his head without answering.

It scared Crawford to see Coe so withdrawn. Coe couldn't go on like this, beating on himself hour after hour.

Crawford stood and let his hand rest on

Coe's shoulder. 'You know I'll be around. We'll just have to wait and see what happens.'

'I don't much give a damn,' Coe said without looking up. That lost note in his voice was a scream for help, and Crawford couldn't do anything about it.

Crawford walked to the cell door. 'I'll keep in touch with you, Coe.'

If Coe heard that, it didn't register enough to even lift his head.

CHAPTER TWELVE

Kincaid paced his office, his hands opening and closing. He couldn't get a firm grip on his scattered thoughts. Every time he thought he had hold of one of them, somebody would enter the office and scatter his thoughts again. He felt trapped, and a fear nibbled at the edges, threatening to grow and devour him. The fear started when he first heard Coe Dahmer was alive. It had taken effort to keep from screaming a denial. Coe Dahmer couldn't be alive. Hadn't he checked on him? But not closely enough, a derisive, inner voice jeered. Coe only looked like he was dead.

Kincaid beat his hands together. Oh God, why hadn't he made sure? It would have been just as easy to dispose of Coe as he had done with Myra.

Fear took a bigger bite of him. Could Coe have possibly seen him? That unanswered question was driving him crazy. Coe could have regained consciousness as Kincaid reclimbed the slope. Kincaid hadn't stopped long enough to examine him again. But if that was so, why hadn't something been said about it before now? Why was Kirby taking Coe to jail instead of coming after him?

Kincaid wanted to yell against the increasing pressure. He was sweating; he could feel the moisture breaking out on his forehead, and itching rivulets ran down from his armpits. The hollow in his stomach grew, and he was beginning to shake.

He walked to the chair behind the desk and sank down into it. Oh God, everything had been in his hands, then that damned Coe had to be alive. He would never forget his shock when he saw Coe with Kirby. It had taken tremendous effort to throw it off enough to even be able to speak. The moment had offered only a limited opportunity, and he had taken every advantage of it he could. If he had been armed, he would have risked shooting Coe, then defend himself because of his terrible loss. A good lawyer could have gotten him out on that, but he didn't have a gun with him. He had tried to kick Coe to pieces, and Kirby had stopped him.

He transferred his rage to Kirby. If Kirby hadn't interfered, he and the others would have taken care of Coe then and there.

His hand trembled as he reached for the desk drawer. He shook his head and pulled his hand back. If he took that bottle out, it would be his fourth drink this morning. Drinking himself into a stupor wouldn't solve anything.

'Come in,' he yelled. Damn it. Another interruption. He hadn't had a full ten minutes to himself since he had walked in here.

Westhoff came in timorously, his face mournful. 'I haven't had time before to tell you how sorry I am about Mrs Kincaid.'

Kincaid tried to match Westhoff's expression. He supposed this would go on until every Bannock Stage employee came in to awkwardly express his feelings.

'Thank you, Westhoff,' Kincaid said gravely. 'I still can't believe it happened.' His face twisted with anguish. 'Oh God, how can I go on?'

Westhoff shifted uncomfortably before Kincaid's misery. 'I know it's hard, but you have to bear up, Mr Kincaid.'

Kincaid screamed inwardly. How many more times today would he have to listen to such drivel? Westhoff was a doddering fool, and his usefulness was behind him. Myra should have fired him, two or three years ago. She had kept too many such employees on the payroll. She looked at their length of service rather than their ability to do a competent job. Kincaid had a lot of such dross to clear out once he was able to put his attention to the matter.

Kincaid kept his face composed. 'I know, Westhoff, I know. But it doesn't make it any easier to bear. What makes me frantic is to think that the man who caused it will probably go scot-free.'

Westhoff rubbed his shoulder. It still ached from Kirby's blow. 'I wish Kirby hadn't stopped us,' he growled. 'We could've taken care of Coe right there. I used to consider Coe as a friend. All of us did. Not any more. We all remember Mrs Kincaid's kindness. Believe me, it won't be forgotten.'

Kincaid stood and took Westhoff's arm. He steered him toward the door. His nerves were stretched taut already. If he had to listen to Westhoff for another ten seconds, he knew he would throw him out.

Westhoff still wanted to talk. Kincaid said, 'You'll have to excuse me. There's so much to do.'

'Sure, sure,' Westhoff said hastily. 'I just want you to know I'm behind you all the way.'

'Yes, yes,' Kincaid said as he pushed West-hoff through the door. He watched him leave with baleful eyes. The doddering old fool. Now, he needed that drink.

He hurried to his desk. One thing he had learned. Coe didn't have a friend left, working for the stage line. Everybody's hate toward him was open and naked for what he did to Myra.

Kincaid's face brightened as he sat down. From what he heard, the feeling of hostility toward Coe was spreading all over town. That was a positive fact. If he put some thinking on it, it could be built up to his advantage.

He pulled out the bottle and was pouring the drink when a voice from the doorway said, 'Pour me one too, honey.'

It startled Kincaid. He hadn't closed that damned door. Some of the liquor spilled onto the desk top. He couldn't stand to listen to more of the drivel Westhoff had spewed out.

He was too absorbed in his thoughts to recognize the voice. He looked up, and his eyes went wide. 'Damn it, Belle,' he said petulantly. 'You shouldn't be here. Not now.'

She laughed softly. 'Why not? You don't have to sneak around any more.' Her tone held a mocking note. 'Don't tell me you're grieving over your loss. You might make all the others believe that, but not Belle. She knows you too well.'

Kincaid stood, his face hardening. She was too sure of herself. Her attitude screamed that. She had no hold on him. She had been well paid for all her favors.

'What will people think, if they see you here so soon?' he asked angrily. 'It proves one thing; that you're not so damned smart.' He was working himself into a high pitch of rage and couldn't stop. 'Out of common decency it seems you'd wait a little while.'

Her face stiffened, and her eyes narrowed under the criticism. She looked like a dangerous cat, ready to spit and claw.

'Ah,' she said softly. 'Things have changed.'

She didn't seem nearly as attractive as before. 'It has, Belle. I'll see you when things settle down.'

'I get it,' she snapped. 'You'll come after me when you're ready.'

Kincaid blinked at the fury in her tone. His face was outraged. Who in the hell did she think she was, talking to him like this?

'You seemed to have called it right, Belle,' he said stiffly.

Her nostrils were pinched together with

the rush of her breathing, and her bosom rose and fell. 'Why, damn you,' she said shrilly. 'All of a sudden, you're a big man; too big for the likes of me.'

'Maybe you've called it right again,' he said coldly. What had ever possessed him to find this woman desirable. 'Why in the hell don't you just get out of here?'

Her face turned ugly under the ravage of raw passion. Kincaid was quite sure she was going to curse him. If she opened her mouth again, he'd take pleasure in throwing her out of his office.

Belle whirled and flounced toward the door, her shoulders a stiff line of outrage. She turned there and looked back at him. 'We'll find out who made the mistake,' she spat. 'You'll be glad to come crawling after me.'

'Oh, get out of here,' he said wearily.

CHAPTER THIRTEEN

Kirby shook his head as he looked at Coe's untouched tray of food. 'Damn it, Coe,' he said. 'You didn't eat much yesterday. Are you going to start that over again?'

'What do you want me to do, Jude, stuff it down? Food sticks in my throat.'

'Okay,' Kirby sighed, as he picked up the tray. He paused before he left the cell. 'Anything I can get for you?' He knew the answer would be negative before Coe shook his head. Coe didn't want anything. He just sat there, staring broodingly into space. Kirby had never seen anybody so battered by his own thoughts. Could a man drive himself crazy by that bitter introversion? Kirby didn't know; but he knew he would be glad when Coe was off his hands, one way or the other. He hoped Tim Anderson got back this morning. He wanted a smarter mind than his, to give him a decision about what he was involved in. Had he been overzealous in arresting Coe as prime cause of the accident? He had been pretty worked up when he first heard about it, but after serious reflection, he wasn't so sure. He hoped Anderson could straighten him out.

He walked into Anderson's office, and Anderson was putting away some papers in his desk. He was a big, rawboned man with hands the size of hams. He was rough enough to whip a bear barehanded. He was equally as rough mentally. Tucson would never know a better prosecutor.

Anderson rubbed those prominent knuckles across his beard stubble. Evidently, he had just gotten in and hadn't taken time to clean away the marks of his trip.

'Hello, Jude,' he said in that booming voice. 'I was pretty sure I'd see you this morning.'

'You don't know how glad I am to see you,' Kirby exploded.

Anderson grinned. 'What's the matter, Jude? You get hold of a wildcat and can't let go?'

'Something like that,' Kirby admitted wryly. 'You've heard about what happened here?'

Anderson's grin disappeared. 'I heard about it, Jude. I was damned sorry to hear about Myra.'

'So is everybody in town,' Kirby said

gloomily. 'Every place I go, I see and hear people talking that something should be done.'

'But you're not so sure,' Anderson said.

'I was at first, Tim. But not any more.'

Anderson sat down and hooked his heels over the desk's edge. 'Let's have your version, Jude.'

'Coe admits he was drunk the night before the accident. Hell,' Kirby said unhappily, 'I can get fifty people to attest to that. Coe had three drinks the following morning. Now he's pretty sure he was drunk all over again. He's convinced it was the liquor that made him drive over the edge. Tim, I'm telling you he's dead inside. He just sits and stares at nothing. He's eating himself up with his thoughts.'

Anderson nodded grave agreement. 'I can imagine. I know how he felt about Myra. Now you want to know what to do with him?'

'I sure do,' Kirby said and sighed. 'I'm convinced he didn't do it deliberately. But is there some charge that fits the situation?'

Anderson pulled at an ear lobe. 'You want me to name that charge?'

Kirby brightened. 'That's it, Tim.'

'I wouldn't touch this one with a ten-foot

pole,' Anderson said positively. He held up his hand at the argument forming on Kirby's face. 'I know how a jury would go if this came up before them. But it would never get as far as a jury. I don't think Judge Harmon would even consider a private hearing.' A trace of argument still remained in Kirby's face, and Anderson said patiently, 'What are you going to base it on, Jude? A lack of moral responsibility? There's no laws to cover something like this.'

'Damn it, Tim. It just doesn't seem right that nothing can be done.'

'I agree with you,' Anderson said crisply. 'Some day, society will pass laws covering moral responsibility. But so far, it hasn't happened. Damn it, Jude, if moral responsibility was the basis for arrest, half of the town would be locked up, including you and me.'

'Then what do I do with him?' Kirby asked helplessly.

Anderson shrugged. 'Turn him loose. What else can you do?'

'In a way, I'm glad you feel that way,' Kirby said. 'Just looking at him was driving me crazy.' He turned to leave and Anderson stopped him.

'When's Myra's funeral?' he asked.

'This afternoon,' Kirby replied.

'Then I'll give you a piece of advice. Don't let Coe out today, maybe not even tomorrow. Give the town time to simmer down. People always do after the first shock.'

Kirby stared at him with troubled eyes. Anderson sounded so cold-blooded, but then he was probably right.

'I'll do that,' Kirby said and left the office.

He walked back toward the jail, his thoughts heavy and depressed. Maybe Anderson was right when he said the town would simmer down, but things would never be quite the same. He was sure Coe would never be.

Kirby looked in at Coe before he settled down for some necessary paperwork. Coe just sat there with the same blank look on his face.

Kirby decided against telling him he was going to release him in a day or two. Maybe it would be best to break it abruptly when the time came.

'Feel like eating now, Coe?'

Coe shook his head.

'All right,' Kirby said. 'Just let me know when you are.'

He started to turn away, and Coe stopped him. 'Jude, when is Myra's funeral?'

138

Kirby was tempted to say he didn't know, then changed his mind. He could never look Coe in the eye if he lied to him about this.

'This afternoon, Coe,' he said quietly.

Coe's face hardened from some inner determination. 'I'm going, Jude. Even if I have to break out.'

Kirby's temper flared. This was about as ridiculous a thing as he had ever listened to. Coe didn't have any say-so in this. He looked at Coe's face, and his temper faded. Coe might not be able to make this threat come true, but he could sure raise a lot of hell. After what had already happened to Coe, Kirby didn't want an additional burden placed on him.

'Listen, Coe–' he started.

'You listen to me,' Coe said fiercely. Unshed tears sparkled in his eyes. 'Jude, can't you see? It's the last thing I can do for her.'

Kirby was a practical man. He wanted to ask what good that would do Myra. He could add a half-dozen more reasons why Coe shouldn't even think of going. Instead, he sighed and said, 'It could cause a lot of trouble, Coe.'

Coe's determination didn't weaken. 'I'm going,' he said firmly.

Kirby gave in before that unshakable determination. Coe had already gone through too much hell. Maybe he had this right coming to him, maybe it would ease a little of his torment. Besides, hadn't Anderson informed him he had no legal basis to hold Coe any longer?

Kirby's words belied his scowl. 'All right, Coe. If that's the way you've got to have it, I'll take you.' His scowl increased in intensity. 'But you're coming back here with me. Do you understand that?' This was only for Coe's good.

'Jude, I'll never be able to make this up to you,' Coe said earnestly.

Kirby might be wrong, but he thought some peace was touching Coe's face. It filled him with a small wonder, at the same time arousing his anger. This big, dumb ox! Coe wanted to say something else.

'Why don't you just keep still?' Kirby snapped.

Kirby's attention wasn't on the funeral oration. He was too tense, and his eyes shifted from face to face. Myra was well liked. He would guess two hundred people were attending the service. He was well aware of every black look thrown Coe's way, but so far nobody made a physical move toward Coe. Maybe the solemnity of the moment held people's worse natures in check.

Coe stood beside Kirby. He was tense too, but for an entirely different reason. His hand were clenched, and his face was an inscrutable mask. But the late afternoon sun reflected on the sheen of tears in his eyes.

Kirby shifted nervously. It sounded as though the preacher was going to drag out his eulogy forever. The preacher's voice droned on and on, extolling all of Myra's virtues. He had enough of those to work on, Kirby thought glumly. He just wished this was over; he wished he had Coe away from this crowd.

Kincaid stood across from Kirby and Coe at the graveside. He's making quite a display of himself, Kirby thought in disgust. Kincaid bawled openly; his face twisted out of shape. Maybe his judgment was too harsh, Kirby thought. He didn't have the right to judge the depth of Kincaid's grief.

The eulogy was finally over, and Myra's coffin was lowered into the grave. With the first shovelful of dirt tossed into the grave, Kincaid broke completely. He groveled in the dirt, beating his fists into the ground, he pulled at his hair and howled. People looked askance at this show of grief and pulled away from him.

With all attention drawn to Kincaid, Kirby thought he would never find a better time to leave. He touched Coe on the arm and muttered, 'Time to go, Coe.'

He was pleasantly surprised when Coe nodded. Kirby was afraid Coe would object.

He blew out a breath of relief after they were through the crowd. But his tension didn't ease until they were several yards from the cemetery. Nobody knew when some crazy impulse would seize people.

Kirby and Coe walked back to the jail without exchanging a word. Kirby glanced several times at that sober face beside him. He hoped Coe had found some small relief.

Coe stepped into the cell and said, 'Jett took it hard, didn't he?'

'Too hard,' Kirby said savagely. 'I never saw a more sickening public exhibition.'

'That's being too rough on him, isn't it?' Coe objected. 'He just had so much grief in him he couldn't hold it.'

'Or maybe it was guilt, and he was trying to atone for it.'

That shocked Coe, for his mouth dropped open.

'Maybe he was trying to impress the public

142

with his undying love, but to me it was pure manure.'

Kirby's voice rose as Coe frowned. 'Don't try to tell me I'm out of my head. I've seen him at Belle's a couple of times. Once, sneaking in, the other sneaking out. Are you trying to tell me I'm wrong in guessing at what he was there for?'

At the darkening in Coe's eyes, he said heatedly, 'I don't give a goddamn what a man does personally, but I don't want him trying to convince me he's a saint.'

Kirby held back his snort and stalked away. Coe would sit there for a long time and try to puzzle his way through what Kirby had just said. Coe was pretty thick-headed in a lot of things.

CHAPTER FOURTEEN

'Damn him,' Kincaid muttered for the half-dozenth time. If he didn't stop this pacing, he was going to wear a path in the carpet. He told himself repeatedly that he was foolish to do all this unnecessary worrying, but he couldn't help it. It had been a minor shock when he heard Kirby let Coe go. He didn't know what the charge would be, but he had hoped Coe would be locked up at least for a short time. Even six months would have been welcome, for it would be enough time to forget all about Myra.

'Damn him,' Kincaid said again, and smashed his fist into his palm. 'He was guilty. He drove over the edge.'

It gave him a start to realize he was beginning to believe that story himself. He had listened to so many people who did feel that way it was beginning to have its influence on him.

He laughed shakily. He had put on quite a show at the cemetery; everybody was convinced how great his loss over Myra's death was.

'Except maybe Coe,' he muttered. If Coe wasn't fooled, what had he told Kirby? The fact Kirby released Coe was highly alarming.

Things couldn't have gone better. Only one annoying fly remained, and that was Coe. That fly buzzed around Kincaid's head until he wanted to howl against its persistence.

Kincaid bit off the end of a cigar and jammed it into his mouth. But Coe couldn't know, he argued with himself. But what if Coe had regained consciousness long enough to see him around the wrecked stage? Kincaid had scoffed at that assumption a thousand times, still he couldn't completely deny its possibility.

He chewed through his cigar and savagely threw it across the room. Kirby must believe no guilt could be laid at Coe's door. If that was so, would Kirby be looking elsewhere?

That was the question that was driving him wild. All of his worries should have been buried with Myra, but he was sweating as hard as he ever had.

'Damn him,' he muttered again. He wished Coe was dead. How many times had that futile wish tormented him. If only he

145

dared just shoot Coe. Enough people would believe his grief drove him to it except one. Kirby was the important one. He could wreck all of Kincaid's dreams and hopes.

Kincaid couldn't stop playing with the vicious thought of getting Coe out of the way. Could he hire somebody to do it? There was danger in that, too. No matter how much he paid whomever he hired, there was the risk of that one becoming dissatisfied and asking for more money.

Kincaid groaned. He was between the jaws of a vise, and they seemed to be inexorably closing in on him.

He made another turn around the room. Why did Coe stay around here? Outside of Bill Crawford, everybody detested him. That hating should be enough to run Coe out of town but not him.

'I'd like to set fire to his ass and run him out of town,' Kincaid muttered.

His eyes widened. 'That's it,' he exclaimed. 'Fire!' At the very least, Coe would be burned out of Crawford's place. If Kincaid was really lucky, Coe might not get out alive.

Kincaid's agile mind seized on the bare bones of the idea and fleshed it out. Crawford's house was old. With a little help, a fire could get a tremendous start. 'Kerosene,' he said aloud. Five gallons of kerosene should turn that house into an instant inferno. Kincaid's eyes gleamed as he thought of Coe waking up with a fire in his face. There would be no real danger to him. If he waited until after midnight, nobody would be around.

Kincaid banged his fist on his desk. 'It'll work,' he said fiercely.

Coe pushed back his plate after a few listless bites.

'You're not eating much,' Crawford said.

Coe's attempt at a smile was as dead as his eyes. 'Not hungry, Bill.'

Coe's haunted look worried Crawford. All the way from the jail he had tried to get Coe to open up but with little success. Coe had crawled into a hole and pulled it in after him.

Crawford stood and took the coffee pot off the stove. Coe's cup didn't need much refilling.

Coe barely sipped at his cup, then set it down.

'I know I'm not the best coffee maker in the world,' Crawford said in mock indignation. 'But it's not that bad.'

Even that feeble joke didn't lighten Coe's expression.

Crawford wanted to beat on him, anything that would snap him out of this horrible lethargy.

He kept a hand on his temper and tried to talk to Coe again. 'I was sure glad to see you turned loose, Coe. I knew they didn't have anything they could make stick.'

Again, Coe gave him that odd, strained glance. 'Did you, Bill?' he asked dully. 'You knew more than I did.' He shook his head. 'It just doesn't seem right.'

Crawford had Coe talking, but the trend was all wrong. 'What doesn't seem right?' he demanded.

'Somebody should pay for what happened to Myra,' Coe said despondently.

Crawford wearily shook his head. Dear God, this wound didn't go deep into Coe; it went all the way through him. He was sick unto death of listening to Coe berate himself. Coe wasn't going to let anybody, including himself, forget that he had been driving that stage.

Crawford blew out a hard breath. 'Coe, I've known some pretty smart men. Not one of them could change in the slightest way what has happened.'

Coe blinked at the vehemence in Crawford's tone. 'You trying to say something to me?'

Crawford's voice rose to a shrill pitch. 'You're damned right I am. Those smart men didn't waste a second trying to change the past. They put all their effort on the future. They could do something about that.'

Coe was silent, but he didn't look angry. Crawford dared hope he had gotten through to him. Maybe he had jarred Coe out of the deep rut his own misery had worn.

Coe shook his head. 'This is different, Bill. I can't put it behind me as easy as you say. I killed somebody who meant a lot to me. All because—'

Crawford crashed his fist against the table, interrupting Coe. The dishes jumped and clattered. 'For Christ's sake,' he shouted, 'I've heard all this before. I know how you felt about Myra. Are you going to go on beating yourself the rest of your life? Then I advise you to lay in a lot of clubs so that the pleasure you seem to enjoy won't be interrupted.'

Affronted, Coe stared at him. 'I don't know what you're talking about.'

'Then you're more stupid than I thought you were,' Crawford snarled. 'My God, Coe, you're the last man I ever thought would turn himself into a martyr. You go

149

right ahead and enjoy it. Make yourself a bigger mess than you already are. I'm sick of hearing about it. I'm going to bed.'

All the way to the door, Crawford waited for Coe's outraged howl of protest. It didn't come. Coe had retreated so far that it was impossible to reach him.

Coe shook his head as he watched Crawford leave the room. He wasn't angry at him. Crawford just didn't understand.

He sat there a long time, his thoughts moving as though they sloughed through heavy, sticky mud. He couldn't help but feel some resentment toward Crawford. Bill had lived long enough to know that one way or another every man had to pay for his mistakes.

'He just don't understand,' he muttered, and got to his feet. He might as well try to go to sleep, though from the experience of the past few nights, the prospects weren't good. He wanted desperately to slip into the oblivion of sleep and quit this damned thinking that wracked him.

He blew out the lamp and left the room. Crawford was the lucky one, he was already snoring when Coe entered the bedroom.

Coe undressed in the dark, not wanting to disturb Crawford. He lay there seemingly forever. Sleep taunted him, coming close, then mockingly retreating just as he was sure he was going to close his hands on it. He fell into a jumbled mixture of half-wakefulness, half-sleep. The sleeping periods were laced through with frightening nightmares. He would awaken from them, his mouth dry, his hands shaking. Some of those nightmares were so real they scared him. It took a long time for sleep to come after that.

He didn't know when he drifted off into sleep again. He was driving the stage again, and he was reliving every vivid second before he drove off the edge. Only this time he was falling straight into roaring flames. He screamed in animal terror. There was nothing he could do to avoid those flames. He was getting closer and closer to them. The crackling of the flames filled his ears, and he could smell the heat from them. This was the worst of all the nightmares.

He was sitting upright in bed when his eyes flew open. He was sweat drenched, and his lungs heaved as though he had been running for a long time.

'It was only a nightmare,' he muttered. He needed the assurance of the sound of his own voice.

Coe stared about the room, needing the

sight of familiar objects to reorient himself. He remembered the room was pitch black when he closed his eyes. He felt like whimpering as he thought, the nightmare wasn't over yet. The room was filled with an eerie, red light that seemed to grow then wane. The nightmare wasn't diminishing, if anything it was growing more real. Coe was sure he heard the crackling of flames, and the air in the room was heated. Oh God, he moaned. He was back in the midst of that terror.

His breathing clogged in his throat as he realized this wasn't some sleep-induced figment of his imagination. This was reality. The house was on fire. By the volume of the light and roar of the flames, the fire had a tremendous start.

Coe jumped out of bed, fumbled about for his pants and boots. He didn't take time to dress. In just the few seconds since he had been fully awake, the light had grown stronger, the roaring louder.

He hurried over to Crawford's bed. Crawford still snored, completely unaware of what was going on. Coe grabbed a shoulder and roughly shook him awake.

Crawford stared dazedly up at him, spluttering, 'What – what–'

'The house is on fire,' Coe shouted. 'We've got to get out of here.'

Crawford's eyes were still heavy with sleep, and even that startling announcement didn't get through to him.

Coe wanted to swear at him. He shook Crawford again, rougher this time. 'Get up,' he screamed. The light in the room had a rosier hue. He could smell the smoke, and he thought he heard timbers of the house creak and groan.

'Damn you,' Coe said fiercely. 'Do you want to lay there and burn up?'

Crawford finally understood what was happening, for he whispered, 'Oh, Jesus.' He crawled out of bed, but his movements were fumbling, his eyes vague.

'Come on, come on,' Coe said impatiently. Already, it might be too late for them to get out. Wind blew flame across the window, blocking that egress. The heat had built up noticeably.

'Gotta save something,' Crawford mumbled.

Coe thought he knew what motivated Crawford. A man, faced with the loss of everything he owned, felt a frantic need of saving something.

Coe grabbed two blankets off Crawford's

153

bed and stuffed them into Crawford's arms. 'Save these,' he said.

He pushed Crawford toward the door. The parlor was a sea of flames. They couldn't get out through the front door. Coe turned toward the kitchen, pushing Crawford ahead of him.

The fire didn't seem quite as fierce back here, but flames were beginning to lick around the back door. Coe glanced upward at the ominous, shuddering groan. He could swear the ceiling was sagging. In a matter of seconds, he thought the house would collapse.

He jerked the blankets from Crawford and put them over Crawford's head. 'Don't fight me,' he yelled in Crawford's ear. 'I'll steer you. You just keep moving.'

He pointed Crawford toward the door. Coe kept his hands on Crawford's shoulders to keep him headed right. Oh damn, it seemed as though Crawford merely crawled, but then Coe had to remember that Crawford couldn't see.

Coe ducked his head and closed his eyes just before they reached the doorway. Now, it was only a black hole in a wall of fire. He sucked in a deep breath, heavy with smoke and heat. If they could get through that doorway, a few more yards would carry them safely outside. He prayed he didn't lose his sense of direction.

The heat was terrible. Coe was sure his skin was shriveling under it. Something crashed across his shoulder, and he wanted to yell at the fiery pain. He kept shoving against Crawford, trying to will more speed into his feet. His lungs threatened to burst. He needed a breath of air. Instinct warned him that if he took it, he would take in nothing but fire.

Coe burst through the doorway, pushing Crawford ahead of him. His eyes were still closed, but exploding bursts of red kept shooting behind his eyelids. His head was reeling. Coe knew he couldn't take another step without breathing.

The stale air left his lungs in one great exhalation, and he breathed in fresh air. The air was still hot, but not nearly as bad as it had been back there.

Coe dared open his eyes. They were outside the house; they were through that flaming doorway.

He looked dazedly about him. They were a dozen yards from the house. He pushed Crawford on, but that terrible sense of urgency was gone. He sucked in breath after breath and didn't stop until the air was cool.

His shoulder hurt like hell, pulling his attention to the burned spot on his underwear. The material still smoldered, and he beat out the creeping line of fire. The exposed flesh was inflamed and puffy. A falling brand must have brushed his shoulder, as he went through the doorway.

Little glowing spots appeared in a half-dozen places in the blankets that covered Crawford, and Coe pressed his thumb on them and extinguished them.

He pulled the blankets off of Crawford's head and said in a choking voice, 'We made it.'

Crawford looked at him big-eyed, then stared at the house behind them. 'My God,' he said, unable to find other words.

Crawford shook visibly, and his tongue refused to work. He finally managed to say, 'I didn't think we were going to get out of that.' Comprehension filled his eyes. 'You saved my life, Coe,' he whispered.

Coe draped a blanket over Crawford's shoulders. The night air had a bite to it. A few seconds ago, they had been close to burning up, now they were shivering. 'We were lucky, Bill,' he said gravely.

Coe put on his pants, sat down, and tugged on his boots. His teeth chattered, and he wrapped the other blanket around his torso.

Crawford stared mournfully at the burning house. 'Everything gone,' he muttered. 'It sure went up in a hell of a hurry.'

Coe nodded. He had been thinking the same thing. His mind picked at something he couldn't quite grasp. That fire had gone too fast, or else, it had been burning a long time before it awakened him.

Watching a fire consume everything a man owned had to be the most depressing sight he would ever see. It left him feeling so helpless and lonely. The fire was attracting attention, for he heard faint cries and saw distant running, dark figures.

Help was on its way, but it was coming a little late, Coe thought dully. The fire drew his eyes with horrible fascination. The house was definitely swaying. The fire-weakened timbers were beginning to give way. The timbers creaked and groaned, and the sharp cracks of breaking wood sounded frequently. The house couldn't stand much longer.

The breeze veered and blew into Coe's face. It carried the heat of the fire and something else, a pungent, unpleasant smell. Coe

157

sniffed at it. He thought he had smelled the same odor before he got out of the house.

He started to ask Crawford if he smelled the same thing. The house suddenly collapsed wiping out his question. It fell with a rending and tearing of wood, and for a fiery instant, the flames leaped higher and higher, sending dancing plumes of sparks far into the air.

'Oh Jesus,' Crawford said, his distress naked in his voice.

Coe guessed at what Crawford was thinking. He put an arm across his shoulders. Crawford had lived in this house longer than he had. Crawford had to feel a terrible sense of loss.

The flames burned more fiercely, then began to die sullenly. The yelling voices were close now, but Coe didn't turn his head. It wouldn't make any difference. If all of the town was here, nothing could be done, for nothing was left to save.

Kirby was one of the first arrivals. He barely glanced at the burning remains of the house. All of his attention was on Coe and Crawford.

'You two all right?' he asked gruffly.

'Just fine for a man who has lost his home,' Crawford said with macabre humor.

Kirby made an impatient gesture. 'You know what I'm talking about.' He peered at Coe. 'Man, you were too close to it. Your shoulder's burned, and your hair's singed.'

Coe gingerly touched his cheek. The skin was painful to touch. 'I feel it,' he admitted. 'I woke up just in time to get out.'

'What made it go up like that?' Kirby asked.

Coe sniffed again. 'Jude, do you smell something odd?' The same pungent smell remained in the air.

Kirby sniffed and shook his head. 'Just a lot of heat. What do you mean–' He broke off, his eyes widening. 'Hell yes, I smell something.' He groped for a word to describe the smell, and Coe waited. He wanted Kirby to name it.

'That's kerosene,' Kirby cried. 'You can't mistake that smell. This fire was set. Who would want to do that?'

Coe shrugged. 'Probably any of a hundred people you could name,' he said wearily. He grimaced. 'I'm not the most likeable man in town.' He flared at the skepticism in Kirby's face. 'I know it was set because of me. Bill was just caught because he took me in.'

Kirby pursed his lips as he stared speculatively at him. He didn't argue with Coe,

159

but he wasn't in full agreement, either. 'I'll take a look around the house,' he said.

'You go,' Coe said in a tired voice. 'I'm too beat to move.'

Kirby nodded and walked away.

More and more people arrived, bunching several yards from Coe and Crawford.

Not a damned one of them had any real sympathy, Coe thought dully. Besides the morbid curiosity that had drawn them, they probably felt a fiendish delight that Coe was burned out.

'It's getting cold,' Crawford said.

Coe looked at him dispiritedly. He didn't know what he could do about that. He didn't know of a single place that would take them in. 'Where shall we go?' he asked in a dead voice.

'To the shop,' Crawford answered. 'I've got some old clothes there. It'll get us out of this wind.'

'Do you want them to burn down the store, too?' Coe snapped. Whoever was behind this had burned down Crawford's house; they wouldn't stop here. There was no reason to think they wouldn't try again.

Before Crawford could answer, Kirby reappeared. He was carrying something.

Kirby held up the tin container as he

160

neared them. 'There's no doubt about the cause now,' he said grimly. He shoved the container under Coe's nose. 'Smell this.'

Coe didn't have to. He knew what that tin had contained.

'What good does that do now?' Coe asked dejectedly.

'It might give me something to go on,' Kirby said grimly. 'How many places in town sell kerosene? I'll find out who bought it.'

'If you do find out, Jude, I'd like to know,' Coe said. His voice picked up new life.

Kirby glanced queerly at him and shook his head. 'I'll do what is necessary, Coe.'

CHAPTER FIFTEEN

Kincaid stood in deep shadow some two hundred yards from the burning house. He breathed hard, and he couldn't take his eyes off of the fire. This fire exceeded his wildest expectations. But then, it should have taken off with five gallons of kerosene splashed about.

He was so tense with anticipation that he ached physically. A growing sense of jubilation grew within him. At any moment, the house should fall. Coe wasn't going to get out of that. No man could possibly get out of that inferno.

Kincaid couldn't believe his eyes. Two figures were running out of the house. 'Goddamn it,' he half-shouted. He was sick with rage and disappointment.

He beat a fist against a thigh. 'That lucky bastard.' His sense of triumph was gone, leaving him feeling empty and futile.

People were beginning to arrive on the scene. Kincaid knew he should go now, but still he lingered. His hopes were going as fast as Crawford's house.

Kirby was one of the first arrivals. 'He got here in a hurry,' Kincaid muttered. He wanted to see what Kirby would do.

Kirby and Coe were talking. Kincaid wished he could hear what they were talking about.

He stirred restlessly as Kirby started away from Coe. Where was Kirby going? Kirby gave the house a wide berth as he skirted it. What was he looking for?

'Kirby doesn't know anything,' Kincaid said to himself. Kirby had to do a certain amount of nosing around to impress people. Kincaid's anxiety grew more pronounced. The fire was pulling more and more people. Few of them, if any, had any sympathy for Coe's predicament, but just the same, it wasn't the wisest thing to be seen near here.

Kirby was coming back. For a moment, Kincaid couldn't make out what he was carrying. Then his eyes widened in near panic. He cursed himself for discarding that kerosene tin; he cursed Kirby for finding it.

Kincaid had to discipline his runaway thoughts. In his anxiety to get away from the house as fast as he could after he splashed on the last of the kerosene, he had tossed the container away without further thought.

Kincaid stared at the tin Kirby showed to Coe, appalled at his stupidity. Finding that container would be conclusive proof to Kirby that this was no natural fire. That would set Kirby's bloodhound nose to quivering. He wouldn't stop until he learned who had recently bought kerosene.

Kincaid groaned in anguish. He saw all the flaws in what he had once thought was brilliant thinking. He had taken several drinks when he thought of burning Coe out. Those drinks hadn't helped him, either.

'You stupid fool,' he muttered. He had left tracks as wide as Main Street. He had to move in a hurry to wipe them out.

His jaw was set in a hard jut. He had to get to Dieckman in a hurry. He couldn't allow Kirby to question Dieckman in the morning about who had recently purchased kerosene. The thought of further violence scared Kincaid, but there was no other course left to him. A sob rattled in his throat. At least, he had been thinking enough to bring a gun with him.

Kincaid thought of Coe, and his face twisted. Coe must have a charmed life. Kincaid had taken two cracks at him and missed both times. Coe had come out of them, practically unscathed. On each occasion,

164

Kirby had taken a hand. Was it some kind of a warning? Kincaid shivered. There wasn't going to be a third try against Coe. If he could get out of this sorry night, Kincaid was going to let Coe alone. Besides, he had a business to run.

Kincaid felt that odd shiver again. It was almost as if tonight was some kind of a supernatural warning.

He turned, and his stride lengthened. He would erase this sorry mistake, then forget all about Coe. He had let his desire for revenge against Coe blind him. It wouldn't happen again.

Dieckman's house was on a dark and lonely street. He was a widower and lived alone. Kincaid looked all about him before he walked up to the door. He didn't expect to see anybody because of the late hour. Besides, anybody who was out would be drawn to the fire.

He rapped on the door, waited impatiently a few seconds, then rapped louder. The old fool! Couldn't he hear?

He pulled the gun out of his pocket as he saw a lamp lit. The sound of footsteps grew louder. Kincaid drew a deep breath. The tension gripped him with a physical force.

Dieckman opened the door and peered

out. He held the lamp in an upraised hand. He was a short, pudgy man, and he hadn't stopped to put on his glasses, for he peered nearsightedly at Kincaid.

'Yes,' he said, the petulance of interrupted sleep heavy in his voice. 'What is it? Oh, it's you, Mr Kincaid.' He started to move aside. 'Come in, come in.' The petulance was gone from his voice, though a curiosity still remained. What did Kincaid want of him at this hour?

Kincaid stepped in close to Dieckman and raised his hand. For the first time, Dieckman was aware of the gun.

His eyes rounded in horror. He set the lamp on a small table, near the door, his shaking hand almost upsetting it.

'No,' he gasped. 'There is some mistake.'

'There is,' Kincaid said. 'I've come here to wipe out that mistake.' He rammed the gun into Dieckman's belly and pulled the trigger once, then again. The sounds of the reports were muffled by the nearness of Dieckman's body.

Kincaid stepped back quickly to avoid Dieckman's clutching hands. Dieckman tried to scream, but the only sound he could make was a coughing grunt. He hung upright a long moment, his eyes agonized in a stricken face.

Kincaid watched him fall with dispassionate clarity. Dieckman would never tell anybody who had purchased kerosene from him.

He whirled and was almost running as he went down the street. He hoped this nightmare was ended for good. He could see no way in which a finger could point at him. Maybe some good would come out of this night after all. Maybe Coe would leave town. Kincaid hoped so, but he would do nothing more to influence Coe one way or another.

CHAPTER SIXTEEN

Crawford frowned when he saw Kirby's office was empty. Damn it, he couldn't find anybody this morning.

After making an aimless circuit of the room, he sat down. He would wait a few minutes before he left. It seemed as though he was a step behind everybody this morning. Coe wasn't there when he awakened, and now Kirby wasn't here.

He waited what seemed like forever, though probably it wasn't more than ten minutes. He was ready to leave when Kirby came in.

'You don't get down very early, Jude,' he complained. 'Was last night's fire too rough on you?' He missed the hard set of Kirby's face.

'Rough enough,' Kirby said flatly.

'You're not the one it was rough on,' Crawford jeered. 'You lost a little sleep. I was burned out.'

'Worse things can happen,' Kirby said glumly. He sat down behind his desk and stared unceasingly at nothing.

'You just name it,' Crawford challenged. 'Seeing his home burn up is the worst thing that can happen to a man.'

Kirby looked piercingly at Crawford. 'Unless he was shot in the belly. Twice,' he said softly.

Crawford's jaw dropped. 'Naw,' he said in disbelief. 'Who'd that happen to?'

'Old Dieckman,' Kirby said in a weary voice. 'I'd say sometime after your house burned.'

'Who'd want to shoot him?' Crawford exploded. 'I never heard of him harming nobody.' A thought occurred to him, and his eyes narrowed. 'Was it robbery?'

Kirby shook his head. 'I might have considered robbery, if it happened in his store. But he was shot in the doorway of his house. The house wasn't ransacked. I think he opened the door for somebody he knew. He set a lamp on a table beside the door. It was about out of oil when his body was discovered.'

'My God,' Crawford said. 'First, my house burned, then somebody kills Dieckman. You've got a crime wave on your hands. Have you got any idea–'

Kirby cut him short by shaking his head.

'Not the slightest. Nobody ever heard of Dieckman having an enemy. Bill, I'm beginning to believe the man who burned your house killed Dieckman.'

'Is that just a wild guess, Jude?'

Kirby sighed. 'So far, no more than that. But the man who burned your house might not want Dieckman remembering who bought kerosene from him.'

'Then I want to find that bastard,' Crawford said fiercely.

'Both of us,' Kirby grunted. 'Ever since Coe had that wreck, it seems like everything is going to hell.'

'You blaming Coe for the fire and Dieckman's killing?' Crawford asked hotly.

'Oh, for God's sake,' Kirby said in disgust. 'I can't even mention Coe's name without you getting your claws out. Quit being so damned protective of him. All I'm saying is that all the trouble started with the wreck. Didn't it?' He glared at Crawford.

Kirby's fierce expression broke up into a wry grin. 'What are we doing arguing? We're both on the same side. I'm not blaming Coe for anything.'

Crawford was only partially mollified. 'Then you sure as hell have changed.' He grinned wickedly at the flush on Kirby's face.

170

'Damn it, Bill,' Kirby growled. 'I always knew there was no malice in what Coe did. But I had to find out if he had any legal responsibility.'

'So you finally forgave him,' Crawford said. 'That was damned generous of you.'

Rancor was naked in Kirby's eyes. 'I only did what I thought was necessary,' he said stiffly.

Crawford grinned. He had pulled a heated response from Kirby. His face sobered, and he sighed. 'I wish to God Coe could forgive himself. We were talking about the wreck before we went to bed. I got tired of sitting there, listening to him pull himself apart. I jumped all over him.' A reflective frown was on his face. 'Then he saves my life. Damn it,' he burst out, 'I'm not apologizing for losing my temper with him. But what am I going to do with him? He looks at me, and his eyes are dead.'

Kirby nodded somberly. He had noticed the same thing while he had Coe locked up. 'I guess a self-inflicted brand is deeper and more lasting than any society can put on a man.'

They were silent a moment, each occupied with his thoughts. Crawford sighed and said, 'I used to raise constant hell with him about his drinking. Now, I'd be glad to see him tilt up a bottle again.'

Kirby nodded in sympathy. Crawford put that pretty well. In the place of a fun-loving, happy-go-lucky man, Coe was now a ghost.

'How was he this morning, Bill?'

'He was gone when I woke up. I thought he might be here. He should have that shoulder looked after. He got a bad burn. All I had at the shop was a little salve. I told him he should get down to Biddle's and have that burn attended to. He nodded, but I don't think he even heard me. He doesn't hear anything I say.' His face clouded. 'I used to rave at him about beating himself with all that drinking. He's not drinking any more, but now he's getting beat up worse than ever.' He thought of Coe's haunted eyes. 'And not just physically either.'

'Maybe he did listen to you, Bill. Maybe he went to see Doc.'

'I hope so.' Crawford stretched and groaned. 'We slept on the shop's floor last night. I never realized what a comfortable bed I had.'

'I hope things start looking up for both of you.' Kirby never meant anything more sincerely.

'Appreciate that,' Crawford muttered.

'Wish the same thing right back at you. I'll look in on Doc.' He waggled a finger in acknowledgment of the talk with Kirby.

Crawford looked back from the door. Kirby's face was set in a somber study. He was a thorough-going man. He would worry over Dieckman's death, or until time finally convinced him he couldn't solve it. In that respect, he was a lot like Coe. He was harder on himself than any outsider could possibly be.

Crawford's face showed his disappointment when he walked into Biddle's small office. Coe wasn't here.

'Left about twenty minutes ago,' Biddle said in response to Crawford's question. 'I had a lot of work to do on him. That burn needed attention, and I replaced the bandage on his head and retaped his rib. He's a walking wounded, if I ever saw one. If he doesn't give time for some of his hurts to heal, there won't be anyplace left on him for new ones.'

'Those hurts aren't the ones I'm worried about, Doc.'

Biddle nodded agreement. 'I know what you mean.'

'I was hoping he'd open up with you, Doc. Did he say anything at all how he feels inside?'

'He didn't say a dozen words, Bill. He just sat here and stared blankly at nothing. He's not the Coe I know.'

'He isn't,' Crawford said vehemently. 'Will he work out of that?'

'I wish to God I knew. Some men can throw off something like this in a hurry, others carry it the rest of their lives.'

'Oh fine,' Crawford growled. He was afraid he knew which classification Coe fell into. 'Did he say where he was going?'

Biddle wouldn't quite meet Crawford's eyes. 'He didn't say, Bill.'

Crawford eyed him shrewdly. 'But you've got an idea of where he's going.'

Biddle nodded weakly. 'He borrowed my mare. I stood in the door and watched him go. He headed that way.' Biddle pointed to the east.

'Oh, goddamn it,' Crawford swore. Biddle pointed at the road that led toward Brady's Grade. Crawford was sure that was where Coe was going.

'You think he's going to ride out to the scene of the wreck?' Biddle asked quietly.

'I know he is,' Crawford snapped. 'He hasn't had a chance to ride out there before.'

'I wish I knew if it was good or bad for him,' Biddle mused. He met Crawford's challenging eyes. 'Don't ask me, Bill. I don't know what to do.'

'I'm going out there,' Crawford said flatly. 'After I get through unloading on him maybe he'll never speak to me again. But I've got to do it.'

Biddle's hand rested briefly on Crawford's shoulder. 'You know what you've got to do.'

CHAPTER SEVENTEEN

Crawford saw the riderless horse at the crest of the pass before he started up the grade. That was Biddle's old mare, and Crawford wondered where Coe was. Probably Coe had gone down to the wreck, or he was just sitting up there, looking down upon the ruined stage. Crawford hoped it was the former. At least, it would be action of a kind, instead of just sitting up there, staring into space.

As Crawford came out of the switchback, he saw Coe sitting on a rock at the edge of the road. Crawford sighed. Outside of riding up here, Coe hadn't accomplished a thing except to just sit and give himself more hell.

Coe looked around at the sound of hoofs. Crawford wondered if that start was due to a sense of guilt at being caught here.

'Hello, Bill,' Coe said and returned his gaze to the wreck below him.

Crawford swung down. He intended to be calm and rational, and instead he could feel his temper rising. 'You figure this is doing you any good?' he asked caustically.

The cords in Coe's neck stood out like small cables. Crawford had scraped him the wrong way. Coe didn't look at Crawford as he said in a low voice, 'This is the first time I've seen it, Bill.'

Crawford didn't miss the pleading note in Coe's voice. If Coe expected him to join him in his maudlin brooding, he had another think coming.

'You saw it before,' Crawford snapped. 'The day it happened. You getting more out of looking at it again?'

Crawford noted with satisfaction the dull wave of color flowing into Coe's neck. At least, he was accomplishing something, if only making Coe mad.

Coe had a remarkable grip on his temper. 'Bill, you don't understand. I didn't see it too well that day.'

Crawford glared at Coe. Coe didn't look at him. Crawford intended dragging him back to life, or losing the friendship between them forever.

'You can see it now,' Crawford said coldly. He wanted to arouse Coe to anger, even if he bore the brunt of it.

Crawford started down the steep slope, taking small, careful steps, leaning backward against the pull of the descent. He didn't look back, but he heard Coe stand.

'What damned good is that going to do?' Coe yelled after him.

Crawford didn't turn his head. 'I just want to see it up close,' he shouted back. He didn't know whether or not Coe would follow him, and it might only make things worse. Seeing the wreckage up close again might mean the final shattering to Coe's spirit. But that was the chance Crawford had to take. Any action would be better for Coe than just sitting there, wallowing in his misery.

Crawford was a good twenty yards down the slope when a small cascade of pebbles clattered and bounced by him. Coe was following him.

Halfway down the slope, a dozen vultures rose with difficulty from the remains of what had been two horses. They were so gorged they could hardly lift themselves, and they beat their wings frantically.

Crawford barely glanced at the bones. The vultures had almost picked them clean.

He slowed to let Coe join him. Coe's face was chalk white, and he breathed hard. Crawford didn't let the pity he felt for him show on his face.

'Which two horses were those?' he asked casually.

'Dandy and Blister,' Coe answered unwillingly. He scowled at Crawford. 'Did you do any good coming down here and looking at them?' His face was contorted, his eyes squeezed to small slits. A tic had started in his left cheek.

He's reliving it over again, Crawford thought. Maybe I was wrong dragging him through it. But sometimes, a brutal moment like this could jerk a man out of the past and into reality.

'Go back up,' Crawford said harshly. 'I came down to look at the stage. I'm going to do it.'

That's pure hatred in Coe's eyes, Crawford thought uneasily. Maybe he's debating upon slugging me now.

Crawford turned and moved downward. He didn't think Coe would jump him from the rear.

He made the rest of the descent, uneasily aware that Coe was following him. So far, Crawford had a small margin; Coe made no attempt to catch up with him. He heard Coe's hard breathing, sounding like a small, furious wind.

Maybe he'll knock me on my butt when

we reach the stage, Crawford thought uncomfortably. He hoped not. Coe could squash him with one blow. He wasn't sure what he expected to accomplish. Maybe the sight of the stage would unloosen Coe's tongue; maybe he would find words the only way to cleanse his mind and spirit. And maybe not, Crawford thought forlornly. It could also make Coe retreat further into his shell. An improvement in Coe was a forlorn hope at best, but Crawford didn't know what else he could do now.

Awed silence held his tongue as he looked at the stage. He would never look at a worse wreck. He could just imagine the tremendous battering the stage had taken in its plunge down the slope. It must have rolled over and over all the way down. It was no wonder that everyone was killed in this accident. The wonder was that they could even be identified as humans.

Crawford walked completely around the stage. He didn't know what he was looking for, but something kept picking at him. He made another circuit, trying to make out details of this wreckage.

Coe's hand clamped on his shoulder and spun him around. His face was a mask of despair and loathing. 'Are you satisfied now?' he asked hoarsely. 'Goddamn you, I'll knock your thick head off.'

A fist drew back, and Crawford thought, here it comes. This hadn't done Coe any good at all; it had only intensified the awful moments he had gone through the other day.

Crawford made no attempt to defend himself. He guessed he had earned anything Coe felt like giving him. 'Go ahead, Coe,' he said in resignation. 'Do whatever you feel like.'

His eyes widened, and the elusive thing that had been picking at him hit him like a blow. The stage lay on its left side. The two left-hand wheels were smashed and broken. So was the one right-hand wheel. But where was the fourth wheel?

'Hold it, Coe,' he yelped. 'Where's the wheel that's missing?'

Coe stared stupidly at him and slowly lowered his fist. 'What are you trying to say?' he managed.

'There's only three wheels on the stage,' Crawford said impatiently. 'What became of the fourth one? Why isn't it here?'

Coe looked like an idiot. He heard the words, but they didn't make any sense to him. 'I don't know what you mean,' he muttered.

Crawford's impatience grew at Coe's

thickness. 'The stage had four wheels, didn't it? I count only three.'

Coe blinked as he sucked in a deep breath. He looked at the stage, then back at Crawford. Now, he understood what Crawford was driving at.

'The fourth wheel got broken off on the way down here,' he said.

'And maybe not,' Crawford retorted. Coe's eyes were coming alive again; he was beginning to think. 'I think we'd better go find out what happened to that fourth wheel. Damn it, don't you see? Maybe you didn't drive over the edge at all. Maybe that fourth wheel came off and pitched you over.'

Coe paled, and he briefly closed his eyes. Crawford suspected that Coe was praying that he was right.

'Let's go see.' Coe said it quietly enough, but there was a new strength in his voice. However, a fear still remained in his eyes, and Crawford could guess at its cause. Coe was afraid they would find a broken wheel farther up the slope. If they did, it would shatter Crawford's theory and ruthlessly trample under the new hope.

They separated a hundred yards and re-climbed the slope, working back and forth

182

like conscientious bird dogs. Every now and then, Coe would stop and stare intently all around him, covering more ground with his eyes. A wheel was a large object and not easily overlooked.

Crawford didn't dare speak until they reached the top. God forgive him if he further strengthened a false hope, but he went ahead and said it anyway. 'I didn't see it,' he said flatly.

'Me neither, Bill.' A new note of confidence was in Coe's voice. 'Bill, I'm beginning to think—'

Crawford interrupted him. 'Don't go jumping at anything yet.' A frosty grin broke up the tough façade of his face. 'But I will say the picture's beginning to look different.'

Crawford moved slowly along the edge of the road, his eyes fixed to the ground. Coe spoke to him, and Crawford waved him quiet. He wasn't sure what he was looking for, but he didn't want to be disturbed.

Coe walked beside him, not saying anything.

'Ah,' Crawford said triumphantly. He pointed to a short furrow gouged deeply into the ground. 'What would you say made this?'

Coe stared at the gouge. The color left his

face, but the sick despair was gone from his eyes. Instead, they had a new blaze in them.

'Bill,' he said. He spoke slowly to be sure of his control over his voice. 'If a wheel came off, the axle end would make such a gouge.' He took a long, careful breath, then the air burst from his lungs in an elated explosion. 'Bill, I didn't drive over the edge. A damned wheel came off. I wasn't responsible.'

'It sure looks that way,' Crawford replied. His eyes were dancing, and his solemn expression was fading. 'Let's check it out a little more. Maybe we can find that wheel and prove it beyond doubt.'

'Let's get at it,' Coe said, a new eagerness in his voice.

Crawford shook his head as he followed Coe. It was amazing how a man's whole personality could change in the matter of a few seconds. All that was needed was to remove the heavy mental weight crushing him.

They spent a good two hours before they found the wheel. Crawford had been up and down that cursed slope until his legs trembled. There was no telling how far a wheel would roll after it came off an axle; there was no telling where that wheel would be.

Crawford groaned as Coe started down again. His legs screamed in protest with each step. But Coe wouldn't give up now; not until he found the wheel.

Coe stopped suddenly, his face ablaze with triumph. 'There,' he shouted.

Crawford sobbed in relief. That was a flash of color lodged halfway down behind a stunted tree. He peered at it until his eyes watered. As far as he would tell, that flash of color was red and black, the colors the Bannock Stage Line used on its vehicles. Whatever that color was, it was out of place down there.

'Could be,' he grunted.

Coe whacked him on the shoulder. 'I know it is,' he shouted, a new vibrancy in his voice.

Crawford moaned at the thought of another trip down that slope. 'Let's go see,' he said grudgingly.

They slithered and slid their way to the stunted tree.

Long before they reached it, Crawford could see that a wheel was lodged against the tree.

Coe stared at the wheel a long while before he looked at Crawford. His face looked as though it would break up, and Crawford

thought, oh God, what's wrong with him now?

'I didn't kill her,' Coe said. His voice was low but remarkably calm.

'That's what I've been trying to tell you all along,' Crawford grumbled. 'But you wouldn't listen.'

The sparkle was back in Coe's grin. 'You miserable, old bastard. I'll always be eternally grateful to you. You drove me into looking.'

'I can't claim much credit for that,' Crawford said soberly. It was awesome how little pieces kept fitting together until a whole picture emerged. Coe could thank himself for riding out here to look at the wreckage. Crawford could thank himself for getting so mad at Coe that he tried to yank Coe out of his misery-ridden lethargy.

Crawford looked up at the top of the crest and groaned. It seemed such a long way up there. 'Let's be starting, though you'll probably have to carry me most of the way.'

'Don't plan on it,' Coe said, shaking his head. 'I want to get this wheel to the top.'

Instant alarm flooded Crawford's eyes. 'Coe, it won't do any good. The town won't believe it. This won't prove anything to them.'

'It'll prove something to me,' Coe said savagely. 'You go ahead. I can manage.'

Crawford cursed him in flat, dispassionate words. He looked at that stubborn face and moaned. 'It has to be your way, doesn't it?'

'This time it does, Bill.'

It took a hell of a struggle to get the wheel back to the top. The wheel was heavy and clumsy, for it couldn't be rolled. Crawford insisted upon helping. He could be as thick-headed as Coe.

They tugged and pulled at the wheel, straining their guts for each upward foot. Crawford was limp with exhaustion when the top was finally reached. All he wanted to do was lie down and die.

He sank down limply as he watched Coe roll the wheel to a crevice between two big rocks. An ordinary passer-by would never see it.

'Will you tell me what good all that will do?' Crawford yelped when Coe returned.

'I can't now,' Coe said soberly. 'I've got to do some thinking about it.'

CHAPTER EIGHTEEN

Kincaid had more important things to think about than Coe Dahmer. The deeper he dug into the business, the more dissatisfied he was with certain aspects. He had never paid much attention to the details of making a business go. Myra had always attended to that.

Westhoff leaned back in his chair and rubbed his tired, old eyes. He had been going through the books since early morning, and it looked as though Kincaid would never let up on him. Dear God, he was so tired, he wanted to whimper. He had dug out everything Kincaid asked for, and he had tried the best he could to explain every figure he had entered in the ledgers.

'Are you tired, Westhoff?' Kincaid asked sarcastically.

'A little, sir,' Westhoff admitted. His nerves were strung so tight that he wanted to scream under the pressure. Myra had never treated him like this. She had considered him an important part of the business and had treated him so. He could see that the former status would no longer hold with Kincaid. With each hour he spent with Kincaid, he grew more afraid of him.

Kincaid sensed that, for he looked at Westhoff with cruel appraisal. 'Maybe you're getting too old to handle the job right, Westhoff.'

Westhoff jerked as though a hot needle pierced his flesh. He didn't know what he would do if he lost this job. At his age, where would he turn? He had been one of the first employees Bannock had hired when the line was started, and at Brad's death, he guessed Myra thought she inherited him, along with the business. His eyes stung with unshed tears. He hadn't heard Kincaid correctly. That had to be the answer.

His attempt at a smile was only a miserable parody. 'I hope you don't mean that, sir. I'm doing everything I can—'

Kincaid brutally cut him short. 'Spare me the sad story.' He stared at the books and didn't see Westhoff wince. The farther he got into the records, the more displeased he was. Certainly, the line was making money. It took in good sums, but it was also paying out huge sums. Kincaid wasn't at all happy with the net returns.

'What's this item?' he asked, stabbing at a figure in the ledger.

'For paint, sir. Myra saw a chance to save money on it. It's for our annual spring paint up. She always wanted to go into spring with everything looking brand new and sharp.'

Kincaid stared at the figure in outrage. 'My God,' he growled. 'That's a hell of a sum to spend on paint. It's a lot of damned nonsense. Send the paint back. This year, we'll skip the annual spring cleanup you sound so proud of.'

Westhoff ducked his head to hide the growing horror in his eyes. Myra would turn over in her grave if she heard this heresy. She claimed that the appearance of prosperity stimulated business.

'I don't know if I can, sir,' he said desperately.

'You'll do it if you want to keep your job,' Kincaid snapped.

Westhoff was growing frantic. 'But, sir, what if they won't take the paint back?'

'I'm holding you responsible to see that they take it back.' Kincaid enjoyed seeing Westhoff squirm.

'Here's another item,' he went on. 'We're spending far too much money on feed. I want the oat rations for the horses cut in half immediately. That's an order.'

If Westhoff didn't actually wring his hands, he gave that impression. 'But sir, we have the best-fed, sleekest horses in the territory. It was Myra's boast that no horses could compare with ours.'

Kincaid leaned back and surveyed Westhoff coldly. 'There's been a change in ownership, Westhoff. Perhaps you're not aware of it.'

Westhoff made a last feeble protest. 'Sadler would take my head off if I told him something like that.'

'Are you afraid of a damned stable foreman?' Kincaid asked with cynical amusement. 'If you're afraid of him, I'll tell him. From now on, I'm putting this line on a real paying basis.'

Westhoff stared at his trembling hands. 'Yes, sir,' he mumbled. Little beads of perspiration dotted his forehead.

'You'd better get used to a lot of things, Westhoff. That'll be all for tonight. Tomorrow, we'll talk of other needed changes.' Kincaid stood and strolled toward the door.

'There's one other thing you should know,' Westhoff said in a barely audible voice. He was desperately afraid to tell Kincaid this.

Kincaid whirled, his face looking mean.

191

'What's that?'

'Our loan comes due at the bank next week.'

Kincaid felt his throat swelling, tightening his collar. 'What the hell are you talking about?'

'You remember, sir,' Westhoff said frantically. 'Myra borrowed money last year to buy the five new stages. Surely, you remember.'

Kincaid's face was a study in frustration. He knew of the purchase of the new stages, but if Myra spoke of how they had been financed, he hadn't paid close attention. The more he dug into things, the more he learned that Myra spent money with reckless abandon.

'Then pay the damned loan,' he snapped.

Westhoff shook his head. 'I can't, sir. We haven't enough cash reserves.'

Kincaid's fists were bunched so tightly they ached. He forced himself to keep calm. 'What would Myra have done?'

'She would have gone to Mr Shriver and asked for an extension of the loan.'

Kincaid's hands loosened. 'Then there's no problem, is there? I'll ask Shriver in the morning and get that extension. Are there any more problems worrying your little head?'

Westhoff flushed at the mockery. 'I guess not, Mr Kincaid.'

Kincaid stared at him a long moment before he turned and left. He didn't see Westhoff's shaking hand wipe his forehead.

Kincaid's face was black as he walked toward home. He saw now that he should have taken a more positive hand in the running of the business. He had been too content to let Myra run things, and she ran them into a mess. He smiled crookedly. He hadn't realized how prophetic he was when he told Westhoff things were going to change. They would, beginning in the morning. He would see Shriver when the bank opened.

Kincaid followed Shriver into the bank in the morning. He extended a hand and said a hearty, 'Good morning, Mr Shriver.'

Shriver didn't see the hand, or purposely ignored it. He sat down at his desk and offered no invitation for Kincaid to sit down.

'What is it, Mr Kincaid?' he asked in an icy voice.

Kincaid detested this fat, meticulously dressed man. Shriver always looked as though he just stepped out of a barber's shop. Shriver had all the warmth of a cold, rainy morning.

Kincaid's teeth were on edge. This was the second insult Shriver had given him, all in the space of a few moments. Just as soon as he got things on a firm basis, he would take his account from this bastard.

Kincaid kept a smile on his face, though it took tremendous effort. 'I came to talk to you about our loan, Mr Shriver.'

'Good,' Shriver said crisply. That might have been a flicker of surprise in his eyes. 'I'm glad to hear that you're early.'

The smile remained on Kincaid's face, though he felt as though it would crack and fall out. He shook his head. 'I'm not here to repay the loan, Mr Shriver. I want an extension. You see–' He stopped in disbelief. Shriver was shaking his head. 'What does that mean?' he asked hoarsely.

'It means I cannot grant your extension, Mr Kincaid. Though it doesn't surprise me to hear you asking for it.'

Kincaid's legs felt hollow, and he threw out a hand to the desk to support himself. His tongue was thick in a too-dry mouth.

'You would have granted the extension to Myra, wouldn't you?'

That was naked dislike in Shriver's eyes. 'I would have. But you're not Myra.'

'Why, goddamn you,' Kincaid exploded.

He caught himself. 'I didn't mean that. It just slipped out.'

'Don't apologize, Mr Kincaid,' Shriver said dryly. 'What you said fits you. I must insist the loan be paid on time, or–' His pause had a chilling significance.

Kincaid felt giddy. He couldn't believe this was happening. 'Or you'll do what?' His voice didn't sound as though it belonged to him.

Shriver shook his head. Kincaid was sure there was no real regret in the gesture. 'Or I'm afraid I'll have to lock your doors, Mr Kincaid.'

'You can't do that,' Kincaid cried. 'By your own admission you'd have given Myra the extension. I'm only asking the same courtesy.'

Shriver shook his head again, slowly and definitely. 'From what I've observed, I don't think you're capable of running the business, or at least, not the way Myra did.'

Kincaid's face turned mean and ugly. 'What is that supposed to mean?'

Shriver looked at him with distaste. 'I shouldn't have to explain that to you, Mr Kincaid. But if you insist–' He sighed before he went on. 'Myra was a practical, level-headed businesswoman. Her whole life was dedicated to the stage line. She met every commitment. The bank could trust her. Can you say the same?'

Kincaid was shaking so hard inwardly that he was certain it showed. 'I don't understand you. You're not giving me a chance to prove—'

Shriver cut him short with a sharp gesture. 'To further prove your complete unreliability? I'm only glad Myra didn't learn of certain things.'

Kincaid leaned across the desk, his face wild. 'You'll have to explain that.'

Shriver looked at a loathsome creature. 'I saw you coming out of Belle Thomas' house. It was after midnight. Miss Thomas accompanied you. By your parting, I would say she meant a great deal to you. Unfortunately, Myra's commitment to you was placed in the wrong person. Do you understand me now, Mr Kincaid?'

Kincaid was deathly pale. He reached up and ripped at the collar that was choking him.

'Why, you sanctimonious old bastard,' he exploded.

Shriver stood. 'That'll do,' he snapped. His tone was cold enough to freeze ice. 'I must ask you to leave.'

Kincaid turned and stumbled a few blind steps before he whirled around. 'You'll get your money,' he shouted. 'Every damned cent of it.'

Shriver was already reseated. He didn't look up. 'I fully expect to, Mr Kincaid,' he murmured.

Kincaid didn't remember returning to his own office. If somebody spoke to him on the way, he wasn't aware of them. Everything was crashing around him. Nobody was giving him a chance. He hadn't the slightest idea of where he could raise the needed money. His mind clutched frantically at one thought after another, and nothing would come to him. But that old bastard would get his money.

Westhoff looked up as Kincaid came in. Those blank, staring eyes should have warned him, but Westhoff was too filled with his own anxiety. 'Did everything turn out all right, Mr Kincaid?'

Kincaid turned all his pent-up fury on Westhoff. He couldn't say exactly how, but Westhoff had a hand in the ruin he faced.

'I'll tell you how right it is,' he screamed. 'You doddering old fool. You're fired. Do you hear me? You're fired.'

Kincaid stormed into his office and slammed the door behind him. He poured down three drinks in rapid succession. They didn't do anything to clear his thoughts, but they made them more bearable.

He was about to take a fourth drink when a timid knock on the door stopped him. He lifted his head, and his face turned savage again. That was probably that old fool out there, daring to beg for his job back. Kincaid hoped it was. He needed the physical exertion of throwing Westhoff out of the building.

He sprang to his feet and ran to the door. He jerked it open, and Cummings stood there.

Kincaid's expression must have frightened Cummings, for he shrank back. 'Westhoff wasn't here,' he faltered. 'I thought it would be all right to ask you. I wanted to know–'

Kincaid didn't give him time to finish. 'You're fired,' he screamed. His rage made him spit all over his chin. 'Get out of here.'

Cummings' face was ludicrous with shock. 'But why – why–' he stammered.

Kincaid darted toward him. 'Do I have to throw you out?' he yelled. 'I'll gladly do that.'

Cummings whirled and fled. The last Kincaid saw of him was a thoroughly frightened face just before it disappeared through the door.

Kincaid walked back to his chair and sat down. He panted as hard as though he had been running for a long time. He had just gotten rid of another of the worthless ones. The old fool didn't begin to earn his money. I'll fire a lot of that kind, Kincaid thought as he poured another drink. I'll clean out the whole damned place.

He gulped the drink down, then flung the glass at a wall. He was barely aware of the small shattering sound, and he stared dully at the small stain that was beginning to dribble down the wall.

Oh God, he groaned. What was he going to do? The whole rotten world was against him. All he asked for was a chance.

He knew his face was breaking up. He wasn't actually crying, but he felt close to it.

CHAPTER NINETEEN

Crawford found Coe in the shed behind the saddle shop, just standing there staring at the wheel. Ever since Coe had brought the wheel here in a wagon, he had spent considerable time just looking at it.

'Hasn't it talked to you yet?' Crawford asked sourly. He had hoped that finding the wheel would give Coe complete mental freedom, but something else seemed to grab him.

Coe grinned at him. The grin seemed more normal, and his eyes were clear. Crawford thought he could relax. This was the old Coe he knew.

'Just out here doing some thinking, Bill. The nut had to come off first for the wheel to come loose.'

'Brilliant thinking,' Crawford said sarcastically. 'I never heard of a wheel coming off with the nut remaining on the axle.'

'Hey,' Coe said in mock admiration, 'you're smarter than I thought you were.'

Crawford grinned grudgingly. It was good

to see Coe show enough spirit to make a joke, however feeble.

Coe's face sobered. 'What caused that nut to come off? That's what keeps plaguing me.'

Crawford groaned. 'Don't tell me you've found something else to stew over. Stages have lost wheels before. They will again.'

'You're wrong if you're talking about Bannock stages,' Coe corrected. 'My stage was the first to lose a wheel.' He pointed at Crawford. 'Do you know why?' Coe didn't wait for Crawford's answer. 'Because Myra was a stickler for inspections before a stage pulled out. Years ago, she was in a stage that lost a wheel and turned over. She swore it would never happen to a Bannock stage. She was right. It never did. Every stage was thoroughly inspected before it went out on a run. Don't tell me I don't know what I'm talking about. I've tightened enough wheel nuts before I started driving.'

Crawford stared at him, his eyes startled. 'Are you saying your stage wasn't inspected; or that nut was deliberately loosened?'

'It has to be one or the other,' Coe said soberly. He stared at the wheel so long Crawford thought Coe had forgotten he was here.

'I don't know, Bill.' Coe's expression was remote. 'It has to be one of the two. Either carelessness killed Myra, or somebody wanted it that way. I've got to know.'

Crawford shook his head. 'Oh God, you're going to drive yourself crazy if you don't get your head straightened out.'

Coe grimaced. 'You could be right. Rickles always made those inspections. It was part of his job. I'd like to hear what he says about this wheel.'

Crawford's eyes were distressed. 'Even if your guess is right, he won't admit it. He showed he doesn't have any liking for you.'

Coe frowned. 'I think it was because of what happened to Myra, and he blamed me for it. He thought a lot of Myra. Myra made Rickles' mother's death a lot easier for everybody concerned. Maybe Rickles fooled everybody about the way he felt about Myra. But I just can't believe it. I've got to know.'

'You thinking of just going up to him and asking?'

Coe didn't miss the derision in Crawford's voice. 'Something like that,' he admitted. 'I was hoping you'd give me a hand.'

Crawford looked suspiciously at him. 'Such as?'

'I want Rickles to look at this wheel. Maybe the shock of seeing it will jar some kind of an admission out of him. Or maybe something in his face will give him away.'

'How do you think you'll get him here?' Crawford demanded. 'Just the sight of you will make him try to knock your head off. He tried it before.'

Coe smiled grimly. 'He will,' he agreed. 'I'll use whatever force I have to.'

'Don't you realize what you're saying?' Crawford yelped. 'You try something like that, and Kirby will be all over you again. I should think you'd had enough of that.'

'I've got to know,' Coe said quietly.

Crawford groaned. 'Oh damn it. I see there's no way of stopping you. What have you got in mind?'

'Rickles spends a lot of his time at Landerson's saloon. If he's there tonight, I want to pick him up when he comes out.'

Crawford made one last feeble effort to dissuade him. 'What if somebody's with him?'

'Then I'll have to wait for a better time. Bill, you don't have to go with me.'

'You know better than that,' Crawford grumbled.

Crawford shifted uncomfortably. He was getting so damned tired, standing out here. The chilly night air was making his leg ache, too. He should have used his head earlier when he reported to Coe that Rickles was in

Landerson's. He should have come out and reported that Rickles wasn't there. It would have stopped this damned foolishness tonight. Crawford shook his head at his reasoning. It wouldn't have really changed anything. Coe would only try again.

'Is he going to stay in there all night?' he asked querulously.

'Looks like it,' Coe admitted. It was well after midnight. He could appreciate how Crawford felt. He, too, was getting tired and cold.

Two men came out of the saloon. They were in high spirits as they staggered down the street. Coe waited until their good-natured wrangling faded away.

'If he doesn't come out soon, I'm going in after him,' Coe said.

'That'd be damned smart,' Crawford said heatedly. 'Whoever's left in there would be on Rickles' side. You start a ruckus in there, and you'll have Kirby boiling in, in a hurry. If he has to break up a brawl, you know who he'd blame.'

'You're right,' Coe admitted. This waiting was grinding on his nerves.

Another miserable half hour of waiting passed. Crawford's touch jerked Coe's attention back to the saloon door.

'The waiting's over,' Crawford announced. 'He's coming out.'

Coe watched Rickles walk down the street. Rickles wasn't staggering drunk, but he couldn't be called exactly steady, either.

'Time to pick him up, Bill,' he said in a low voice.

'He won't come easy,' Crawford warned. 'He's pretty tough.'

Coe tapped the gun at his hip. 'That's why I brought this along.'

Crawford shook his head. Coe kept digging the hole deeper, and he was determined to push both of them into it.

They caught up with Rickles a block farther down the street. Rickles wasn't aware they were anywhere near until Coe jammed a gun muzzle into the small of his back.

'What the hell?' Rickles said in instant fright. He whirled despite the gun's menace. 'Oh, it's you,' he said, his face turning mean. 'So you're down to robbery now. Why, goddamn you. I'll knock your head off.'

'Don't force me to use this,' Coe said quietly. 'I'm not here to rob you. Just keep moving along.'

Rickles' dislike was plain on his face. The liquor he had downed wasn't helping his mood, either. His jaw was belligerent, and his muscles bunched.

'You can have it either way you want it,' Coe said. 'Come along quiet, and you won't be hurt.' He was tense as he watched Rickles struggle with a decision. He didn't know which way this would go.

'You'll pay for this later,' Rickles threatened.

'Sure,' Coe agreed. He was limp with relief. Rickles had decided to make no further protest for the moment.

Coe knew how lucky they were when they reached the shed without seeing anybody. Rickles showed a final burst of resistance as he reached the door. Some of the liquor fumes had cleared from his mind, for his voice was clear. 'I don't know what you're doing, but I'll be damned if I just let–'

Coe's hard jab with the gun muzzle broke up Rickles' words. He was tired, and tension made his muscles ache.

'Get in there,' he ordered. 'I told you nothing would happen to you, unless you insist.'

Rickles swept Coe's face with a glance and decided he meant what he said. 'Just wait,' he said belligerently, but he stepped inside the shed.

'Light the lamp, Bill,' Coe said. 'I left one on the bench this afternoon.'

'You thought of everything,' Crawford said sourly. He hoped Coe was right. If he wasn't, there was no way of getting out of the bind this night's action would put them in.

He struck a match and found the lamp. He touched the match to the wick, but the faint illumination wasn't enough to chase all of the shadows out of the shed.

'Bring it with you, Bill,' he said.

The light advanced as Crawford moved across the shed. It picked out the wheel leaning against the wall.

'Recognize that, Ben?' Coe asked softly.

Rickles stared at the wheel, then turned a puzzled face toward Coe. 'It's a wheel. I still don't see—'

'A special wheel,' Coe corrected. 'It came off of the stage Myra died in.'

Rickles' eyes widened as he recognized the familiar coloring of the wheel. All the truculence was gone. He fumbled for words, then said shakily, 'Even if you're not lying, what has this got to do with me?'

'The other three wheels on the stage were smashed in the wreck,' Coe said gravely as he put away his gun. Rickles didn't seem to notice his motion. 'Crawford will tell you. This wheel was found quite a way from the stage. It rolled there after it came off.'

Rickles stared bewilderedly at Coe. He still wasn't following him.

Rage suddenly distorted Coe's face. 'Why, damn you. You and all the others blamed me for driving over the edge. This wheel is the answer to what really happened. It came off and pitched the stage over. I wasn't responsible for the accident. You were!'

Shock widened Rickles' eyes. 'You're trying to put it all on me. You miserable liar. I had nothing to do with it.' He worked himself up into a fury. 'If you think I'll stand here and take that—'

'Shut up,' Coe snapped, stopping Rickles' furious outpouring of words. 'I'm not claiming you wanted it that way. But you were responsible. You didn't make the usual inspection of the stage. You didn't catch a nut that need to be tightened.'

Rickles shook his head. 'No, no,' he repeated over and over. His face was pale, his eyes glazed. 'You're saying I caused Myra's death.' His voice grew more and more shrill. 'I knew Myra was going to be on that stage in the morning. Why hell, I took particular pains to see that everything was all right.'

His eyes filled with horror at the judging in Coe's face. 'I checked every nut. None of them could have worked loose.'

'It's only your word,' Coe said softly.

Rickles appeared close to the breaking point as he searched for words. 'You think my carelessness is responsible, don't you?' His face cleared as he thought of something. 'I can prove I made that inspection. Cummings came up while I was making it. He talked to me while I checked the last two nuts.'

Coe's eyes were troubled as he exchanged glances with Crawford. Rickles' words had the ring of truth in them. Coe couldn't find fault in a single word, or in any of Rickles' reactions.

'You don't believe me, do you?' Rickles asked.

'I think I do,' Coe said slowly. 'Your story would be too easy to check with Cummings. You see what this means, don't you, Ben?'

The horror was growing in Rickles' eyes, and it left him a broken man. 'You mean somebody deliberately unloosened the nut?'

'Can you figure it any other way?'

'Why, this means somebody wanted Myra dead and deliberately set out to do it. My God, man. This is monstrous.'

'It is,' Coe agreed simply.

'Who would do that?' Rickles' voice was little more than a whisper.

'That's what I intend to find out,' Coe said

grimly. 'Ben, I don't want anything said about this. Whoever did it must think he is secure. I don't want him alarmed.'

Rickles looked at the wheel again. 'Oh my God,' he said. His eyes were fierce again as he looked back at Coe. 'I want to help on this.'

'If I find any way, I'll call on you,' Coe said. 'Sorry I had to bring you here like this.' He grinned twistedly. 'But you wouldn't have come here any other way.'

After a moment of thought, Rickles said, 'No.' He paused before he said awkwardly, 'I'm sorry too, Coe, for misjudging you. But I thought–'

'How could it be otherwise, Ben? Both of us hurt over Myra's death.'

He walked with Rickles to the door of the shed. 'Just keep quiet about this.'

'How can a man be so wrong, Coe?' Rickles paused, then said, 'I'd like to buy you a drink. It won't make up for anything, but it'll make it easier on me.'

A faint shudder ran through Coe as he remembered all those anguish-filled hours. 'Not now, Ben,' he said.

'I hope you find the one who did it,' Rickles said fiercely.

'That makes two of us,' Coe responded. 'I'll let you know, whatever happens.'

CHAPTER TWENTY

Crawford stood in the doorway of the shed with Coe, watching Rickles walk away. 'You believe him?' he asked.

'I do,' Coe said sharply. 'Don't you?'

Crawford grinned. 'Yes, I do. I just wanted to see how you felt. Where do we go now?'

'We'll talk to Cummings in the morning,' Coe replied.

'Why, damn it,' Crawford yelped, 'I thought you believed Rickles.'

'I do,' Coe said flatly, 'but we're following a pretty dim trail. I'm hoping Cummings can shed a little more light on it. Have you got a better suggestion?'

Crawford considered that, then shook his head. 'I guess not.' His tone had a cutting edge. 'Besides, it gives you a good chance to check up on Rickles.'

'That was in the back of my mind,' Coe admitted. 'We'll see Cummings after noon today. He doesn't go to work until four o'clock. I don't want to talk to him at work.'

'You got a particular reason?' Crawford

asked softly.

'Not yet,' Coe said slowly.

Cummings lived in a beat-up house at the edge of town. He let things go to hell after his wife died a year ago. Coe was surprised to find him puttering around the yard.

'Hello, Sam,' Coe greeted him. 'I wasn't sure you'd be up this early.'

Cummings looked unfriendly, and he didn't answer Coe.

He still feels like all the others, Crawford thought. Maybe that can be changed. He didn't see how, but he could hope.

'I got to bed earlier last night than I usually do,' Cummings finally said sourly. He seemed unusually depressed.

'Why was that, Sam?' Coe asked.

'Kincaid fired me last night.' Cummings ripped out several oaths, his face showing his passion. 'For no reason. He fired West-hoff, too. I think he's lost his mind.'

Coe's breathing quickened. 'Surely, he had some reason, Sam. Was he displeased with your work?'

'No,' Cummings said stubbornly. 'I think Doc Biddle ought to look him over. Kincaid hasn't been the same since Myra died.' He quickly averted his eyes.

'It affected all of us,' Coe said gravely.

'You oughta know,' Cummings growled.

He started to move away, and Coe checked him. 'Do you remember the night before Myra's stage pulled out in the morning?'

'Why?' Cummings asked suspiciously. He was filled with resentment and sore at everybody.

'Rickles said he talked to you while he was checking the wheel nuts. Did he?'

'He did,' Cummings said grudgingly. 'We talked a little, while he finished his inspection. Why?' he demanded.

'Nothing, I guess,' Coe said and sighed. As far as he was concerned, Rickles was in the clear. 'Did anything unusual happen that night?' he was fumbling now and he knew it.

'That son of a bitch was out in the yard later that evening.'

'You mean Kincaid?' Coe's pulses picked up an odd beat of increased excitement.

'I don't know anybody who better fits that term,' Cummings said bitterly.

Coe's eyes gleamed. 'Was he different then?'

'That's the hell of it,' Cummings exploded. 'We exchanged a few pleasantries. That was all. He wasn't sore at me, then.'

This wasn't leading any place, but Coe hated to let go of it; this was the only thread he had. 'Was Kincaid near the stage?'

Cummings shook his head. 'No, not that I know of. When I first saw him, he was near the tool shed.'

This could be important, though Coe didn't yet know why. 'What was he doing?'

Cummings shrugged. 'Just standing there. But I did find something odd after he left.'

The alarm buzzed and increased its clamor in Coe's mind. 'What was that?' he asked carefully.

'I was in charge of the tools in the shed,' Cummings said bitterly. 'I thought I was doing a good job. I kept every tool in its place. When somebody wanted something, they could walk in and lay their hands on it without fumbling around.'

'Sure, sure,' Coe soothed him. He wanted to yell at Cummings to hurry, but he waited patiently.

'Goddamn him,' Cummings said passion-ately. 'He had no cause to fire me out of hand the way he did.'

Coe nodded his sympathy. 'You found something wrong in the tool shed.'

Cummings spat on the ground. For an instant, Coe was afraid Cummings wasn't going to talk any more. Go on, he screamed inwardly. Go on! He was on the verge of something important, though he couldn't exactly say what it was.

'I walked with Rickles to the shed after he finished his inspection,' Cummings said. 'I watched him put the tool away. After Kincaid left me, I found the wrench Rickles used on the floor.'

Coe carefully spaced his words so that his eagerness would not run them together. 'What time did Rickles put the wrench away?'

Cummings frowned at him. He was growing weary of all these questions. 'Just before dark.'

'When did you talk to Kincaid?'

'After midnight. Maybe a little later.'

'Maybe you just thought you saw Rickles put the wrench away.'

Cummings' face turned red as he glared at Coe. 'Are you saying you think I'm getting too old to remember what I did?' He rapidly worked himself into a passion. 'To hell with you. I didn't want to talk to you when I first saw you. I sure don't want to now.' He turned and stalked away, the set of his shoulders an indignant, squared line.

Coe grinned wryly. 'I sure ruffled his

feathers, didn't I?'

Crawford made an impatient gesture. 'I'll grieve over his hurt feelings later. Did what he tell you lead where I think it does?'

Coe was tight-lipped. 'It could, Bill. But that's all it does. It's no proof of anything. It only says Kincaid had the opportunity of loosening that wheel nut.' He shook his head, appalled at the direction his thoughts were taking him. 'But my God, Bill, it doesn't make sense. Nothing fits at all.'

'Maybe it's beginning to,' Crawford said. 'Who knows what was between Kincaid and Myra? Men have been known to get rid of their wives for one reason or another. Myra's death gave Kincaid the whole business, didn't it?'

Coe shook his head, not in denial of Crawford's argument, but in an effort to straighten out the thoughts that packed his head. This was a monstrous thing he faced, and his mind refused to take hold of it.

'Are you just going to stand here?' Crawford asked impatiently.

'No,' Coe said in sudden decision. This was the first road sign he had seen. Because it didn't make sense, he wasn't going to ignore it. 'I want to talk to Doc about this.' He had to sort out the fragments of his thoughts and see if they could be built into something more solid. He had to go through every little incident since he came to in Biddle's office, and he had been too beaten up to remember them clearly.

Crawford quit trying to talk to him as they walked to Biddle's office. All he got was a grunt, or complete silence. Coe was absorbed with what was going through his mind.

'Yes,' Coe said suddenly. Something hit him with blinding clarity. Kincaid had said something to him when he and the others jumped him while Kirby was taking him to jail. Coe couldn't exactly recall the words, but he was sure Kincaid had yelled something about breaking his head like Myra's was. How had Kincaid known that? Myra hadn't yet been brought in. Had Kincaid been down to the wreck before Myra was removed? That question was a sharp spur, raking Coe.

Biddle looked up as they entered. Their expressions wiped out the greeting he intended to say. 'Something bad?' he asked, his eyes alert.

'I don't know yet, Doc,' Coe answered. 'You saw Myra when she was brought in, didn't you?'

217

Biddle's shudder answered the question. 'She was in terrible shape, Coe.' He paused, then let Coe have it hard. 'Her head was mashed beyond all recognition.' He shook his head in sympathy at Coe's expression of revulsion.

'Would just being thrown out of the stage do all that damage?' Coe asked in a low voice.

Biddle carefully considered the question. 'I puzzled over the same thing, Coe. It seemed to me it would take a greater force to cause that excessive damage.'

'Such as a heavy object being dropped onto her head?' Coe's voice was hoarse and strained.

'That would do it,' Biddle answered. His eyes were narrowed and keen. 'What are you trying to say, Coe?'

'I'm not sure,' Coe said. 'I'll talk to you later.'

Biddle had a dozen questions he wanted to ask, but he had never been a prying man. He would wait until Coe was ready to talk further.

Outside the office, Crawford asked sharply, 'It points only one way, don't it?'

'It looks like it,' Coe said in an ugly voice. His face was pale as he visualized the scene.

Myra was alive after she was thrown out of the stage. But somebody hadn't wanted it that way. That somebody had taken care of the situation.

Coe was thin-lipped. He had the answer as to who was behind Myra's death, but the reason and the proof were lacking.

'The murdering bastard,' he said. 'I'm going to make him pay.' He shook his head at Crawford's expression. He didn't know how, yet.

CHAPTER TWENTY-ONE

Kincaid hardly recognized his own reflection in the mirror. His eyes were bloodshot, his face haggard. The sunken cheeks and the beard stubble highlighted his cheekbones, making them stand out prominently. God, he looked like a death's head. It wasn't possible that he could change so much in such a short time. He shuddered and jerked his eyes away from the mirror. He was going through pure hell, and he didn't see how it could ever get better.

He was afraid to shave this morning, for fear his shaking hand couldn't control the razor. He turned and sank limply into a chair, afraid that his trembling legs would dump him.

Kincaid's mind was a trapped rat racing frantically about, trying to escape. Surely, in a town this size, there had to be a source of ready money he could lay his hands on, but so far he hadn't found it. A dozen futile attempts were behind him. Did increasing failure have its own disagreeable odor? It almost seemed so, for with each turndown, men shrank more and more from him. On the last two attempts, he hadn't begun to get his request out before they were shaking their heads.

Kincaid stared at the floor. He was up against a blank wall, and he could see no way over, around, or through it.

'Damn them all,' he whispered. 'They know their money would be safe. There is no way they could lose it.'

He had offered everything in his possession to get the money he needed, even up to 50 per cent of the business. The filthy vultures were out to strip him of everything.

Kincaid groaned aloud as he thought of his recent failures. He had gambled the last two nights, hoping that luck would smile on him. The first night, he lost two hundred dollars. The second night was worse, mounting to almost six hundred dollars. Now, he was almost out of ready cash. He didn't have to worry about the bank locking his doors. The lack of money to pay for running expenses would do that for him.

He wanted to scream and yell against the unfairness of it all. Such a relatively small sum would carry him over this bad stretch, and no place could he find it.

He pushed from his chair and headed for the bottle, sitting on the dresser. At least, it would blot out the agony of thinking.

Kincaid shuddered and withdrew his hand before he touched the bottle. He had been doing far too much of that lately.

'Goddamn you, Belle,' he shouted. 'You caused it all. If you hadn't come to my office, none of this would have happened.'

In the middle of an oath against her, he stopped, his eyes widening. She was the start of all his trouble, and maybe she could end it. He almost yelled in sudden elation. Why hadn't he thought of her before? Belle ran a profitable establishment. He would offer her a share in the stage line. The temptation of a partnership with him should be more than she could resist.

He pounded a fist into his palm. Here was his solution. It had been before him all the time, and he had been too blind to see it.

He looked at his soiled clothing with distaste. He couldn't go see her, looking like this. Yes, and he needed a shave. Excitement pumped through his veins, almost making him giddy at the prospect of success. It seemed it had been forever since he had known success of any kind.

Despite all his care, he cut himself while

shaving. It was only a minor annoyance, not enough to make him lose his new-found confidence. Nothing could upset him now.

He dressed with meticulous care. Standing before the mirror, he adjusted the cant of his hat with a tap of his fingers. He approved of his appearance; he knew how Belle would react.

This time, he used the front door of Belle's house. There would be no more slinking in and out of the back door. Now, he didn't give a damn who saw him.

He stopped a bosomy blonde and asked, 'Flora, is Belle in?'

A thinly veiled curiosity was in her eyes, but she didn't voice it. 'She's upstairs. In her office.'

He climbed the stairs and looked back. Flora was watching him. His blood raced at the thought of a new prospect that suddenly occurred to him. The two businesses could be merged. He could participate in this business, too. A self-pleased smile spread over his face. How her eyes would widen when he offered her marriage.

He tapped on the door, then opened it without waiting for an invitation.

Belle looked up from her desk, her expression angry. 'Don't you wait to be asked in?'

she snapped.

Kincaid guessed she hadn't recognized him in her first glance, for her face softened. He was filled with the heady aroma of success. Tonight was his.

Belle tilted her head to one side and gave him a long, level appraisal. 'Well, if it isn't lover boy,' she drawled.

Kincaid smiled with complete assurance. 'For a moment, I was afraid you didn't know me.'

'Should I?' she asked coolly. 'The last time I saw you, you almost threw me out.'

A pained expression crossed his face, and he made a deprecatory gesture. It disturbed him that she didn't rise and rush to him, but he refused to let the worry lodge in his mind.

'I didn't know what I was doing, Belle. You must know the strain I was under.'

'And you aren't now?'

The small worry began to grow in him. She seemed so cold, so remote. He wouldn't let his confidence be shaken. Whatever bothered her could be straightened out.

His laughter had a boyish ring. 'I'm not now,' he repeated. 'All of that is behind us, Belle.' Kincaid drew a deep breath as he advanced toward the desk. His next words would melt her; she would fling herself into his arms.

'Belle, I've come to ask you to marry me.'

He waited for the disbelief to fade from her face to be replaced with radiance. The room seemed to have developed a chilly draft. 'Don't you understand, Belle? I'm offering you a full partnership in the Bannock Line.'

He willed the chilly draft to go away. She hadn't realized what he was offering her.

'No other reason that you want to marry me?' she murmured.

Kincaid laughed again. Now she understood. The whole dazzling prospect was bewildering her. 'No other reason.' Now, she would jump to her feet and rush to him.

Shocked outrage spread over his face as she threw back her head and laughed. Peal after peal rang out, and she couldn't stop.

She finally got her laughter under control. 'Why, the honor overwhelms me,' she said mockingly.

Kincaid felt as though all the solid ground had been cut from under his feet. 'Belle – you don't understand,' he stammered. 'You didn't hear what I said.'

She stood, and her face was icy with contempt. 'Do you think I'm as big a fool as you are? It's all over town how desperately you need money. Did you think I wouldn't hear about it? As a last resort, you came here. You poor, damned fool. You thought the offer to make me a respectable woman would sweep me off my feet.'

She threw back her head and laughed again. The obscene sound rolled out in wave after wave, and Kincaid thought she would never stop. His face turned an alternate red and white, and his tongue was so thick it couldn't form the words he wanted.

'Stop that,' he finally managed to shriek. He stared at her wild-eyed. Nothing was going to stop that horrible laughter.

He rushed around the desk and slapped her viciously, first on one cheek, then on the other. Her head rocked under the savage blows.

'I told you to stop that,' he yelled.

The blows stopped her laughter. She fell back a step, but she wasn't afraid. The outlines of his fingers were on both cheeks before they slowly faded under the rush of color.

'You'll live to regret that, Jett.' She looked like an enraged cat, as she spat her last words at him. 'I promise you that.'

Kincaid stared at her in horror. He knew if he didn't get out of here, he would beat her face into a pulp. He whirled and ran to the door. That obscene laughter started again. It rang in his ears as he slammed the door behind him.

CHAPTER TWENTY-TWO

Coe lay on a cot in the rear of Crawford's saddle shop, his hands locked behind his head, staring at the ceiling. It was getting dark, and still he had not arrived at a definite conclusion. There were a lot of fragments, all pointing toward Kincaid, but were they enough to go to Kirby and lay the bits and pieces before him? He decided he didn't yet have enough. Kirby would only scoff and say, 'You're only guessing, Coe. Nobody will believe you.'

Coe scowled and shifted restlessly. Why, would Kincaid want to murder Myra? Coe had gone back and forth over that question a hundred times and came up with nothing definite. Could it be for the business? That wouldn't hold water. Kincaid already had the business, at least, half of it. Maybe he wanted it all, Coe argued with himself. That argument was full of holes. Coe was stymied until he could come up with a solid reason whereby Kincaid would profit from Myra's death.

He heard Crawford come into the room. No matter how softly Crawford tried to move, the gimply leg always gave him away.

'You asleep, Coe?'

Coe answered him with a grunt.

'Thought you'd be hungry by now,' Crawford said.

'I'm not,' Coe answered irritably.

'Don't snap my head off,' Crawford said in an injured tone. He pulled up a chair and sat down beside the cot. 'Haven't come up with anything yet?'

'Just a lot of guesses,' Coe said moodily. 'Not enough to go to Kirby with. The first thing he would ask is what reason did Kincaid have? That would nail me to the wall. There isn't a single reason I can see why Kincaid would want Myra dead. Damn it, I saw them together too much. There was no friction between them.'

'It sure looks that way,' Crawford agreed. 'He showed how much he was hurting over her death, at the cemetery.'

Coe's feet hit the floor with a thud. He cursed his contrary memory. It had a trick of hiding a vital piece of information just when he needed it the most.

'What bit you, Coe?'

'Something you said. And something I just

229

remembered. Kirby was rankled over Kincaid's display of grief. He thought the display was false. Particularly after Kincaid had been visiting Belle Thomas.'

Coe heard the change in Crawford's breathing. It quickened as though Crawford was startled.

'Do you think Kirby was right, Coe?'

'Why would he have any reason to make up that kind of talk?' Coe demanded. 'Maybe that's what I've been looking for. Belle could be the reason Kincaid wanted to get rid of Myra.'

'It's possible,' Crawford said dubiously. 'But it seems to me you're reaching a long way. If it's true, it could be enough reason for Kincaid. But how are you going to find out?'

'Ask Belle,' Coe said harshly as he stood.

Crawford shook his head. 'Belle wouldn't tell you a damned thing unless she wanted to. She'll laugh in your face.'

'That could be,' Coe conceded. 'But I'm going to find out.' He started for the door.

'Wait for me,' Crawford said querously. 'I've been in this all the way. You don't think I'm going to miss the windup, do you?'

'Let's get moving,' Coe said impatiently.

They walked a block in silence. 'If she confirms what you're thinking, are you going to Kirby?' Crawford asked.

'Maybe I'll have to,' Coe said. His voice roughened. 'Even though I'd like to take care of Kincaid myself.'

'That wouldn't be wise, Coe,' Crawford said dryly. To him, even at best, it looked as though Coe had gathered together a lot of sketchy points. He knew the town wouldn't believe Coe. Maybe Kirby wouldn't either. If Coe went ahead on his own, he could have a pack of wolves after him.

'We won't have to go to Belle's house,' Crawford said. He pointed ahead. 'Here she comes now.'

'Good,' Coe growled. 'Maybe she'll be easier to handle out here.'

Crawford shook his head. He had his doubts about that. Belle Thomas had her own brand of toughness.

'Hello, Belle,' Coe said as he approached her. 'I want to talk to you.'

'Now isn't that odd?' Belle asked mockingly. 'You never seemed to have much time before.'

Coe's impatient gesture waved away her words. 'Belle, was Kincaid seeing you?'

Her eyes widened. 'Whatever gave you such an idea, Coe?'

231

Coe ignored the frown on Crawford's face. He knew what Crawford thought. Coe was rushing this matter too fast.

'Belle, I want an honest answer,' Coe said harshly. 'Were you the trouble between Kincaid and Myra?'

Her face sobered, and the mockery was all gone. 'Maybe I was, Coe. I was in Jett's office the night before you took the stage out. It was late. I didn't think—' She stopped, and her shrug was expressive. 'Myra came in and caught us.' She made a small *moue* of distress. 'Shall I say it was an embarrassing moment for everybody?'

'That bad?' Coe asked.

Again, there was that fleeting expression of distaste. 'Bad enough that she ordered me out.'

'Ah,' Coe murmured. He could imagine Myra's unhappiness.

Belle met his eyes. 'She took it hard.' Belle hadn't expected her moment of revenge to be handed her so soon. Kincaid was going to be a sorry man. She hoped that in some way he would know it was her doing that the story got out.

'Did you expect anything else?' Coe asked coldly.

'I guess not,' she said and looked at the

ground. 'But that's not the worst of it. But I did want to make it up to Myra in some way. I returned to the office.' The barefaced admission didn't make her flinch. She had slipped back to the door and listened out of pure curiosity.

She paused, picked her next words.

'Go on,' Coe said impatiently.

'They were quarreling when I returned,' Belle said. 'I didn't go in. I thought it would only make matters worse.'

Coe had the feeling she laughed inwardly at him. 'Is there more?' Disgust was plain in his voice.

'A little,' she admitted. 'Myra was furious. She was tongue-lashing Jett. She kicked him out of the business. I heard her say she never wanted to see him again.' She tried to look piteously at Coe, but it didn't fit with the fierce glint in her eyes. 'You know I wouldn't want something like that to happen.'

Coe raked her with a savage sweep of his eyes. 'I'll bet,' he said harshly and spun on his heel.

Crawford had to hurry to catch up with him. 'Damn it,' he complained, 'this old leg won't stand a race any more.'

Coe's glance contained no apology, and he didn't slacken his stride.

Crawford struggled to keep up with him. 'Are you in this big a hurry to get to Kirby?'

'I've changed my plans a little,' Coe said grimly. Now, he could hand over a package to Kirby, all neatly tied with no loose ends dangling. 'First, I'm going to find Kincaid.'

Crawford's eyes showed alarm. 'But, Coe, you said–'

Coe cut him short. 'I know what I said, but what I just heard changed my mind. I'm going to beat hell out of him before I drag him to Kirby. When I get through, he'll be glad to babble everything he knows.'

Crawford looked at the hard set of Coe's jaw and sighed. When Coe looked like that, nobody could say anything that could move him.

Belle watched them leave. Her breathing quickened so that she almost panted. She didn't need Coe to tell her he was going after Kincaid. 'He'll find you too, you bastard,' she said viciously. Her cheeks still stung with the memory of Kincaid's slaps. She was going to be repaid in full. The only trouble was that she wasn't going to be around to see it happen.

She moved slowly on down the street. Some of the passers-by nodded and spoke to her, but they were mostly men. She was used to women turning their faces from her. It never penetrated her armor.

Her eyes widened as she saw Kincaid coming out of the saloon just ahead. She hurried to catch up with him.

'Jett,' she called, stopping him. 'I want to talk to you.'

He turned and waited, the hangdog look on his face lessening. He is a stupid man, she thought contemptuously. Even now, he wants to believe that I've forgiven him.

Kincaid held out a hand to her, a smile on his face. 'My God, I'm glad to see you, Belle. If you knew the torture I've gone through. I lost my head and—'

His words faltered at the unforgiving set of her face. This wasn't the expression of a forgiving woman.

His smile faded, and he asked coldly, 'Why did you stop me?'

'I've got some important news for you, Jett.' She looked more feline than ever. She almost purred with satisfaction.

'We haven't got anything to talk about,' he said sullenly. She only stopped him to gloat over his misfortunes. He half-turned to go.

'You better listen, Jett,' she said. 'I just talked to Coe.'

Alarm stabbed him as cruelly as a knife.

What did she have to talk to Coe about?

'Nothing you talked about could interest me,' he snapped.

'How wrong you are, Jett,' she murmured. 'He was interested to hear that Myra kicked you out.' Her laugh had an evil ring. 'Oh yes, I know. I slipped back to your office door and listened. I heard what she said.'

His face was stunned. 'You told him that?' he gasped.

'Oh yes,' she said. 'It seemed to drive him wild.'

The growing wildness twisted Kincaid's face. 'Why, you goddamned bitch,' he roared. 'I'll break your filthy neck.'

She fell back a step, though she didn't look unduly alarmed. 'With all these people near us, Jett?' she mocked. 'You touch me, and I'll scream my head off. You don't want to raise that much interest in us, do you?'

He cursed her with every foul word at his command, then turned and hurried away. Her laughter followed him until he turned the next corner.

His thoughts were frantic, threatening to drive him into madness. He knew what Coe would do now. He would lose no time in coming after him.

Kincaid tried to calm himself. What difference did it make if Coe did know about Myra kicking him out? It was no proof of anything else. Kincaid sobbed deep in his throat. But it would divert suspicion from Coe and perhaps transfer it to him. If this much had come out, what about the cause of the wreck? It could come out just as easily. He knew now he should have shot Coe when he first saw him coming down the street with Kirby. It could have been done then. People wouldn't blame him, saying it was only his grief-wracked nerves driving him crazy. He cursed himself for all the omissions and commissions he could now see so plainly. Those things no longer mattered. Now, it had to be done. He had to wipe Coe out before he talked to Kirby, or anybody else. Maybe it was too late, but he had to go ahead on the premise that Coe would look for him before he talked to anybody.

Kincaid's mind picked at the problem that would arise after he killed Coe. He thought about one solution after another, as he ran. He could say he feared for his life because Coe threatened him, or that Coe attacked him. None of that was important at the moment. He could come up with a suitable explanation after it was over.

'A shotgun,' he muttered. It was thorough,

and its blast would make sure there wasn't another mistake.

Kincaid was panting hard by the time he reached his house. He snatched the shotgun from its rack and slipped a shell into it. Now all he had to do was to find Coe.

CHAPTER TWENTY-THREE

Rickles glanced up from his anvil at Coe and Crawford's approach, and his face was apprehensive. He laid down his hammer and pulled at his fingers. The night air was nippy, but Rickles had removed his shirt. Only the bib of his leather apron covered his torso. Despite the chill, he sweat profusely.

'Something wrong, Coe?' he asked uneasily.

'Why? Did you expect there to be?'

Rickles blinked at Coe's tone. 'You just look like trouble,' he said glumly. 'By God, there's plenty wrong around here,' he exploded. He blew out the words as though he could no longer contain them.

'Tell me about it,' Coe invited.

'It's Kincaid,' Rickles said, an aggrieved note in his tone. 'Because of Myra, I tried to be with him all the way, but in less than a week, he's torn down more than Brad and Myra were able to build up in years.'

'What's he done, Ben?' Coe asked quietly.

Rickles was filled with a bitter list of grievances, and he had to get them out. 'First, he fired Westhoff, and right after that, Cummings. Neither of them know of any reason why they were fired.' He morosely shook his head. 'What are we going to do without Westhoff? He ran that office.' He glared at Coe as though Coe was at fault.

Coe shrugged. It was the only answer he could make now.

'He's got Sadler wild,' Rickles went on. 'He ordered the oat rations for the horses cut in half. Why, the damn fool. Doesn't he know that horses can't work if they're poorly fed?'

Coe shook his head in sympathy. Once, Rickles was completely loyal to Kincaid because he was Myra's husband. That feeling was dead.

Rickles picked up his hammer and hit the anvil a resounding lick. He had to do something to work off his sense of utter helplessness. 'I just don't know what's going to happen,' he said miserably.

'Maybe things will get better,' Coe suggested.

Rickles snorted. 'Not with Kincaid running things.'

'That could be changed, too,' Coe said. He caught the startled flash in Rickles' eyes but made no attempt to explain his remark.

'Is he in his office, Ben?'

Rickles shook his head. 'He hasn't been since early this morning. I don't know where he is.'

'Thanks, Ben,' Coe said and started to move away.

'You're going to do something,' Rickles cried. 'It's written all over your face. What can I do to help?'

Coe shook his head. 'Nothing now, Ben. If anything happens, you'll hear about it.' That was the gospel truth. The whole town would be buzzing about this night's events before too long.

'Do we have to run again?' Crawford grumbled as he caught up with Coe.

'I guess not this time,' Coe said and slowed his pace.

'It's a good thing,' Crawford said. 'I couldn't keep up any more. This old leg has just about had it.'

Coe grinned briefly but didn't speak.

'Coe, do you think we'll find him at home?'

'That's what I'm betting on,' Coe replied absently. His thoughts were on the coming confrontation with Kincaid. Kincaid would surely buckle under all the facts Coe had accumulated. It didn't matter, Coe thought

241

almost wearily. He had his fists. He could beat Kincaid's admission of guilt out of him.

'Didn't you hear me, Coe?' Crawford demanded. 'That's the second time I've asked you about what you're going to say to Kincaid.'

'Sorry, Bill. I was too busy thinking about it. I haven't got any speech prepared, if that's what you mean.' His face was turned toward Crawford as he walked. 'I'm sure I'll think of something to say when I see him. Even if it's only cuss words,' he finished with wry humor.

Out of the corner of his eye, Crawford saw an indistinct figure step out from behind a bush and point something at them that looked like a broomstick. But Crawford knew better than that.

'Coe,' he shouted. 'Look out!' He flung his body into Coe, hitting him from the side. His frantic desperation showed in the force with which he hit Coe.

Coe didn't have time to say more than a startled, 'What–' when Crawford's weight knocked him down. Crawford fell on top of him.

Just as he hit the ground, Coe heard the blast of a shotgun. Angry, little geysers spouted from the dirt around them, and

Coe felt a sharp stinging in his left arm and shoulder. He felt Crawford's body jerk convulsively and heard a deep, throaty grunt that could have been a broken sob.

Crawford's body sagged against him, a heavy, inanimate weight.

Something hot and sticky flowed across his hand. Coe didn't need the rush of blood to know that Crawford had been hit, and bad.

'Bill,' he cried. 'How bad is it?' Carefully, he disengaged Crawford's weight from him. Coe thought he heard the hard pound of feet running away, but at this moment, that wasn't important.

He laid Crawford on his back in the dust. Crawford's eyes were closed, and a terrible fear seized Coe that Crawford was gone. He shuddered as he looked at the ghastly stain of Crawford's blood on his own clothes.

'Bill,' he cried again, knowing it was useless, that no mere voice could reach Crawford now.

But he was wrong, for Crawford slowly opened his eyes. He stared vaguely about him, then his eyes focused on Coe.

'Hello, Coe,' he said feebly.

Coe almost sobbed with his relief. 'It's going to be all right, Bill. I'll run and get

Biddle. I'll have him here in no time. You're going to be–'

The words dried up, and fear clutched at his throat, for Crawford was shaking his head. The gesture was weak, but determined. He tried to smile, and it turned out only a grimace.

'No good, Coe,' he said.

Coe had to bend his head close to catch the reedy whisper.

'I got it in the side and back,' Crawford went on. 'Biddle can't do me any good.' Sudden anxiety sharpened his eyes. 'Are you all right? I saw him step out from behind that bush. I didn't have much time.'

'I'm just fine,' Coe said steadily. 'I don't want to hear any more talk like you've been giving me. You're going to be all right.'

Again, Crawford shook his head. The gesture was weaker, but the determination was still there. 'Don't worry about it, Coe. It doesn't matter. I'm so damned tired. It'll be welcome to just let go.'

Crawford closed his eyes, and this time Coe was sure that he was gone. He bent his ear close to Crawford's mouth and felt the small fan of his breathing.

'Bill, Bill,' he implored.

Crawford reopened his eyes. 'I hope you

get him, Coe. I can't be sure, but I think it was Kincaid. I only saw a shadow move. Maybe I'd been thinking of him too much, and that name popped into my mind.' He tried to grin again, and again failed. 'I don't think I'm wrong in accusing him. He's got enough to his credit. Everything's going to be all right with you, Coe. You just remember that.'

A long shudder ran through him, and his eyes froze open.

Coe wanted to scream and curse against the fact that inexorably hammered at him. Crawford wouldn't say anything else.

Coe got clumsily to his feet. His arm hurt like hell, but outside of the wince of pain that crossed his face, no other emotion showed. All the crying was inside him, a tearing thing that wracked and shook him.

He looked down at the lifeless face. 'I'm sorry, Bill,' he muttered. It was a poor, inadequate thing, but he couldn't put his loss into better words.

The fire rekindled in Coe's eyes as he thought of Kincaid, and the resurgent anger was a searing flame enveloping him. He had handled this wrong; Coe saw it now. He should have gone straight to Kirby and told him what he had learned. His petty desire –

to get his hands on Kincaid for the misery he caused – hadn't let him think of anything else. That selfish desire had cost Crawford his life.

Coe forced himself back to this moment of reality. Kincaid could be taken care of later. Now, he had to do something about Bill. He thought of lifting and carrying him away, but with his throbbing arm, he knew it was beyond him. Now, he had to get help.

'Bill,' he started, and the wild rush of grief wiped all coherent thoughts from his mind.

He turned and stumbled blindly away. Bill knew that he wasn't deserting him, that he would be back.

Kirby looked up, alarm washing his face, as Coe staggered into his office. He looked at the dangling arm and the massive blood stain on his clothes.

'My God, Coe,' he blurted. 'What happened?'

'A little trouble,' Coe answered and grimaced, both from the hurt in his arm and the hurt in his mind.

Kirby wanted him to sit down, and Coe waved aside the proffer of a chair. He was afraid if he sat down, he wouldn't get up.

'Most of this is Bill's blood,' Coe said in a frozen voice. 'We were ambushed just a few minutes ago with a shotgun.' Only his eyes were alive in that cold, remote face, and they burned with a savage fire. 'Bill threw himself into me, taking most of the pattern in the back and side. I got just a few pellets in the arm.'

Coe couldn't keep his face composed at the sudden twist of anguish. 'Bill's dead. He's lying out there. I couldn't bring him in.'

'Oh damn it,' Kirby said with naked concern. He took a deep breath before he asked a vital question. 'Did you see who it was, Coe?'

'I didn't, but Bill did,' Coe said grimly. 'He gave me a name before he died. If you go bring Bill in, I'll get Biddle to patch up this arm. You can join me there if you want to.'

'I'll join you at Biddle's,' Kirby said quietly. 'Where is Bill?'

'Near Malbert's house,' Coe replied dully. 'If anybody heard the shot, they didn't come.'

'I'll take care of Bill,' Kirby said. 'You need any help?'

Coe bared his teeth. 'I'll make it. Jude, I appreciate your taking care of Bill.'

Kirby waved aside the awkward thanks. 'You weren't the only friend he had.' The concern didn't leave his eyes. 'You sure you

247

can make it?'

Again, Coe's teeth flashed. It wasn't even close to being a grin. He felt lightheaded and unsteady, but he would make it. 'You can bet on it,' he said thickly.

A half-dozen people passed him on his way to Biddle's office. If they said anything to him, Coe didn't hear them.

Biddle's eyes went round as he looked at Coe. 'Not again,' he moaned softly.

'It looks worse than it is,' Coe said. 'Most of the blood you see isn't mine. I've got some pellets in this arm. I'm bleeding, and it hurts like hell.'

Biddle wasn't a man to waste words where there was work to be done. He sat Coe down and split his sleeve. 'You were peppered pretty good,' he said in a dispassionate voice. 'I'll have to dig some of them out.'

'You're the doctor,' Coe replied with a feeble attempt at humor.

He was grateful that Biddle didn't belabor him with a lot of questions. Each time Biddle dug out a pellet, Coe had to clamp his teeth together to keep from yelling.

'With you as a patient, I don't need any others,' Biddle grunted. He dug out another pellet and dropped it into the pan.

Coe guessed he was hanging on pretty

well. He heard the tiny clink as the pellet dropped.

'That's the last one,' Biddle said. 'Now, I'll get that bleeding stopped.'

Kirby came in just as Biddle had finished the bandage. Biddle stepped back and surveyed his work. 'You won't use that arm very much for a while.'

'I won't need it for what I've got to do,' Coe said. He looked questioningly at Kirby.

Kirby nodded. 'Bill's been taken care of. Who did it, Coe?'

'Kincaid,' Coe said flatly.

He was aware of the startled glance exchanged between Biddle and Kirby, and his anger flared briefly. 'Don't think I'm out of my head.' He related all the facts he had gathered. He thought skepticism remained on their faces.

'Don't try to tell me I'm guessing,' he said fiercely. 'Everything fits.'

'Who's arguing with you?' Kirby retorted. 'I can handle it from here on.' He sighed at the stubbornness hardening Coe's face. 'Knew you'd feel that way,' he muttered. He pulled a gun from his waistband and handed it to Coe. 'I saw you weren't carrying one. You may need this.'

Coe nodded as he dropped the gun into

249

his pocket. 'Thanks, Jude,' he said simply.

'Coe, you're in no shape to go,' Biddle cried. 'You can't–' His protest faltered and died as he looked at those fierce eyes.

'Didn't you hear me tell you how Bill died?' Coe said savagely.

Biddle briefly closed his eyes as he nodded. 'I heard you. Wait a minute. I've got some brandy. A stiff shot will help you.'

'I don't want a damned drink,' Coe said fiercely. He switched those savage eyes to Kirby. 'You ready?'

Kirby nodded. 'I'm ready.'

CHAPTER TWENTY-FOUR

Kirby looked at the darkened house and said in a low voice, 'It doesn't look like he's home.'

Coe impatiently shook his head. He didn't want to believe that. If so, it could mean that Kincaid had already run. Coe was too weary to think of facing that prospect.

'He could be asleep,' Kirby said, though the doubt was strong in his voice.

'Damn it,' Coe snapped. 'Do we stand out here arguing about it, or do we find out?'

Kirby's nerves were on edge too, for he looked at Coe, tight-lipped. They could easily have quarreled. Kirby must have recognized that, for he said, 'We'd better go see.'

They walked up onto the porch, and Kirby whispered, 'Better stand to one side while I knock.' Coe's hesitation must have rubbed Kirby's strained nerves raw, for he said in a low, heated voice, 'Do you want him to know you're out here before he even opens the door?'

That made sense, and Coe nodded. He guessed when this was over, he owed Kirby an apology.

Coe pressed against the side of the door, while Kirby hammered on the door. It was loud enough, Coe thought, to wake sleeping people down in the next block.

The silence grew heavier as the seconds dragged by. Kirby raised his eyebrows, lifted his fist, and pounded on the door again. This time, it was with renewed vigor. If Kincaid was asleep in this house, that had to awaken him.

Kirby was ready to knock for the third time when he saw the faint glow of a lamp in the house. 'Woke up somebody,' he muttered.

Coe nodded, his face a strained mask. His arm hurt, and his head ached. Who else could it be but Kincaid? All Coe wanted was for this to be over.

The light, coming through the long, narrow windows on each side of the door, grew stronger, and Coe thought he heard the shuffling of feet. But that could be his imagination. In the shape he was in he was ready to imagine anything.

'Who is it?' a petulant voice demanded through the door.

'It's me. Kirby! Open this door. I want to talk to you.'

'Damn it,' Kincaid said. His voice was thin but audible. 'Can't a man get a decent night's sleep without somebody disturbing him?'

Kirby shook his head as he looked at Coe. Coe thought the doubt was more pronounced in his eyes. If Kincaid had been asleep, as he claimed, he couldn't have been the ambusher.

The door opened a small creak, and Kincaid peered out suspiciously. 'Just wanted to be sure it was you,' he said in a surly voice.

He opened the door wider. Coe stepped ahead of Kirby, shoving hard against the door. Its swinging edge caught Kincaid and knocked him back a step. He almost dropped the lamp he held in his left hand.

That was raw shock in Kincaid's eyes as he looked at Coe.

'Didn't you expect me?' Coe asked sardonically.

It took brutal effort for Kincaid to pull his face back together. 'I didn't invite you in,' he said hotly. He glared at Kirby. 'What the hell are you trying to pull? This is my wife's murderer.'

'We've been all over that before,' Kirby

said wearily. 'Just a few more words with you. That's all.'

He shoved past Kincaid and walked into the hall.

Coe never took his eyes off Kincaid. This wasn't a man who had been rudely awakened. The eyes were too alert, and they watched him with an animal wariness. Kincaid was dressed for sleep, all right. He wore a night shirt, topped by a bathrobe. Kincaid's right hand was thrust into the pocket of his robe. Coe was sure it held a gun. Kincaid had prepared for this as well as he could. If he couldn't bluff his way out of this tight spot, the gun would let him blast his way out.

'I don't see any reason for you two to be in my house.' The outrage was strong enough in Kincaid's voice, but it had a false ring.

'Don't you, Jett?' Kirby said mildly. 'Lots of trouble out there tonight. Somebody tried to ambush Coe and Bill Crawford. He was only half-successful. He got Bill. A shotgun's a nasty weapon,' he finished reflectively.

Coe watched Kincaid closely. Was that a flicker in his eyes? Coe couldn't be sure.

'Why tell me about it?' Kincaid's voice kept going up in pitch.

'It happened not too far from here.' Kirby's

voice held no accusation. 'Just asking everybody around, if they'd seen or heard anything.' He proceeded on to the kitchen.

Kincaid was worried as he looked at Coe. Coe was behind him, and he didn't like that. He decided he'd better follow Kirby. He hurried after him, his bare feet pattering against the floor.

'I'm glad you brought your lamp with you, Jett,' Kirby said. 'Too dark in here to see very well.' His eyes roamed the room, picking out every detail.

Coe thought that was satisfaction in Kirby's eyes as he looked at the gun rack on the far wall.

'Damned, if I haven't got my hands full,' Kirby complained. 'First, Dieckman was killed and now Crawford. I've got a damned murderer on my hands.'

'You're forgetting Myra,' Coe said quietly. 'She was murdered, too.'

That froze Kincaid's face for a moment. He carefully placed the lamp on a table. Coe noticed he didn't remove his hand from his pocket.

'You should know,' Kincaid shouted at him. 'You did it.'

Coe shook his head sadly. 'Not me, Jett. Somebody loosened the nut on a wheel. The

255

three remaining wheels were badly broken in the fall. I've got the other wheel. Why wasn't it smashed?'

A wildness grew in Kincaid's eyes. He didn't gasp, but Coe had the impression he wanted to.

'You're crazy,' Kincaid said hoarsely.

'You wish I was,' Coe murmured. 'Doc Biddle told me Myra's head was crushed. He thinks somebody used some heavy object. He believes she was alive until somebody checked on the wreck.'

Kincaid's breathing quickened until it had a sibilant hiss. 'Of all the goddamned nonsense,' he shouted.

'Maybe,' Coe said calmly. 'But Cummings told me he found the wrench somebody used, on the floor of the tool shed. You know how particular he is about every tool being in its place.'

Kincaid's face was a pasty gray, and his eyes swiveled from Coe to Kirby.

'I don't see why you're telling me all this,' Kincaid said. He couldn't keep the quivering from his lips.

Kirby ignored Kincaid's words. 'Too many odd things been happening lately. Crawford's house was set afire. It looks as though somebody wanted Coe to be burned up, or at least run out of town. The only thing that accounts for Dieckman's killing is that the arsonist didn't want Dieckman remembering who had purchased kerosene from him.'

That surprised Coe, and he looked quickly at Kirby. Kirby's face was impassive. Maybe Kirby had just thrown that in to further shake Kincaid, but the burning could be a part of Kincaid's general pattern.

He looked back at Kincaid. Kincaid's face was falling into ruin, and his breathing was definitely laboring.

'You woke me up just to tell me all these wild guesses?' Kincaid's attempt at bravado didn't come off at all.

'Another odd thing, Jett,' Coe went on remorselessly. 'Belle heard you and Myra quarreling. Myra kicked you out of the business. That must have made you pretty desperate, didn't it? So desperate that you had to get rid of her.'

Kincaid shrank back until his back was against a wall. He looked as though he needed support.

'Why, you're accusing me,' he cried. Kincaid tried to sound indignant and look injured at the same time. Both attempts were dismal failures.

'As for Belle,' Kincaid said, 'who'd believe

that damned whore? She always hated me because I turned her down.'

'That's odd,' Kirby said, looking puzzled. 'I saw you going into her house a couple of times.'

Kincaid's mouth sagged open. He looked as though he had been kicked in the belly.

'Then there's the matter of tonight's ambush,' Coe went on. 'Who told you I was digging around on your trail? Was that ambush supposed to stop me?'

He watched Kincaid carefully, attuned to every change in his face, every nuance in his voice. He was surprised Kincaid stood up as well as he did under this crushing avalanche of evidence.

Kincaid had to lick his lips to lubricate them enough to be able to speak. 'I never listened to so many goddamned lies.' His voice threatened to crack. 'There's not a shred of proof. Nobody would listen to you. Why, they know how much Myra meant to me.'

'You could be right, Kincaid,' Kirby said thoughtfully. 'I tried to tell Coe he could be all wrong. But once he gets a thought in his head, nothing shakes it out.'

Hope washed Kincaid's face. 'I knew you had some sense,' he babbled. 'Coe's always been against me. He knew I was going to fire him.'

'I haven't forgotten,' Kirby murmured. He moved to the gun rack. 'Interesting collection of guns, Jett. Why, here's a shotgun.' He sounded astounded. He picked the shotgun out of the rack. His astonishment grew. 'Why, this one has been fired recently. The barrel's still warm.' He sniffed at the muzzle. 'Smells it, too.'

That completed the ruin of Kincaid's face. His mouth was open as he gasped for air, and he slobbered over his chin.

'Lies,' he screamed. 'all lies.' He struggled to free his hand from his pocket. Something hindered him, for Coe heard the ripping of material.

Probably the sight or the hammer caught, Coe thought with complete detachment. He didn't even hear Kirby's startled yell. Coe pulled the gun from his pocket and leveled it before Kincaid could free his hand. Coe's first shot hit Kincaid at the apex of his rib cage, slamming him against the wall. Coe shot him again, though there was no necessity. The first shot had been for Myra, the second for Bill Crawford.

He looked at the crumpled figure before he turned to Kirby. 'It's done,' he said dully.

Kirby rubbed his hand across his forehead. He breathed hard. 'Yes,' he agreed. 'I didn't know whether or not he would break.'

'I didn't know about Dieckman,' Coe said.

Kirby slowly smiled. 'I didn't, either. It just hit me all of a sudden that it had to be that way.'

His face sobered. 'Coe, I'm going to have to lock you up again.'

That stirred Coe's outrage. 'For what? For shooting that? You were here; you heard it all.'

'For your own safety,' Kirby said calmly. 'You know how this town feels about you. When they hear of Kincaid's death, I don't know what they'd try to do. It's just until I'm sure that everything's straightened out.'

Coe understood, for he smiled wanly. 'I don't care where you put me, Jude. As long as I can lie down. My God, I'm so tired I don't think I can stand much longer.'

'Yes,' Kirby said. 'This kind of a night wears out a man, doesn't it?'

CHAPTER TWENTY-FIVE

Coe didn't want to open his eyes, but somebody insisted upon awakening him. He recalled so many other mornings Bill Crawford had shaken him awake, and he almost said, 'I'm awake, Bill.' All those other mornings were forever gone, and the cold clarity of the moment hit Coe hard.

He opened his eyes and squinted up at Kirby. 'What time is it, Jude?'

'Almost noon. I looked in several times. I thought you were dead.'

Coe sat up and groaned at the numerous twinges of hurt the movement started. 'Almost wish I was,' he grunted.

He paused a moment before he asked, 'Does the town know about last night?'

Kirby nodded. 'The people know.' He anticipated Coe's next question and said, 'They took it with shock and stunned surprise. Then a lot of them got mad, remembering how Kincaid had fooled everyone. A few flatly refused to believe it could be true. They claimed Kincaid wouldn't do the things I said he did. I think some of those hard heads will go to their dying day, still firmly convinced you drove over the edge and killed Myra.'

At the distress showing in Coe's eyes Kirby said, 'They don't matter, Coe. There's always the fringe that no one can convince of anything. Just consider yourself lucky that most of them can see how it all happened.'

Coe nodded soberly. He guessed Kirby called it right. He was lucky.

Coe swore softly with the effort of getting his boots on. That left arm gave him pure hell. It hurt with the slightest pressure put on it.

He finished the chore and looked up at Kirby. 'How in the hell does a one-armed man get on his boots?'

Kirby grinned. 'I hope I never have to find out. Breakfast?'

Coe shook his head. Breakfast was too steep a hill for him to think of climbing now. 'I could use some coffee,' he admitted.

'Thought you could. I put it on the stove before I came in to wake you. It should be hot.'

Coe smelled the aroma before he walked into the office.

At his grimace, Kirby asked, 'Something wrong?'

'I just remembered how godawful your coffee is,' Coe said soberly.

Kirby grinned good-naturedly. 'You go to hell.'

Coe finished his second cup. 'As bad as your coffee is it makes me feel almost human.'

'You sure don't look like it,' Kirby retorted.

Coe rubbed the back of his fingers across his beard stubble. He imagined he looked pretty rough. He couldn't fault Kirby for that remark. He weighed the effort of shaving and gave up the thought with little struggle. That was another hill he couldn't face right now.

'What are you going to do?' Kirby asked.

Coe sighed. 'I wish to God I knew.'

'Oh, I almost forgot. Shriver wants to see you, as soon as you can get down to the bank. I let you sleep it out,' Kirby said, 'but by now, Shriver must be pacing around his desk.'

Coe frowned. Shriver had never been one of the people he wanted to be close to. Shriver was straight-laced. Coe could guess Shriver would be called one of the moral

263

pillars of the community.

His frown increased. 'I don't know why he wants to see me. I've never had a dime in his bank. He probably wants to raise hell with me to point out the error of my ways.' Coe snorted. 'To hell with him. He can't snap his whip at me.'

Kirby thoughtfully regarded him. 'Shriver's an influential man in this town, Coe. I believe I'd go see what he wants.'

He saw the familiar stubbornness setting on Coe's face. 'Would it kill you to find out what he wants? If you don't like what he says, you can turn and walk out, can't you?'

'Oh, come on,' Kirby said impatiently as Coe's expression didn't change. 'Maybe it's about time to listen to a few people.'

Coe gave in. 'I'm not sitting there, listening to any sermon from him,' he warned.

'Maybe you won't have to. I've got to go that way. I'll walk to the bank with you.'

Coe eyed him suspiciously. Kirby's face was sober enough, but that could be a glint of amusement in his eyes.

Kirby left Coe at the bank's door. Coe was beginning to regret he had agreed to come.

'I look pretty rough to walk in there,' he argued.

'Hunting excuses to get out of it?' Kirby

gently mocked him.

Coe swore at him and stalked into the bank. He wasn't afraid to see anybody. Maybe Shriver wouldn't get out a half-dozen words before Coe walked out on him.

Coe was surprised to see Shriver rise at his approach and extend a hand. Coe reluctantly accepted the handshake. Maybe his guess about Shriver was wrong, but all of his suspicion didn't abate.

'Sit down, sit down,' Shriver said cordially. 'Bad thing that happened last night.'

Coe grunted. Here it came. He was too damned forgiving to agree to come down here. He sat on the edge of the proffered chair.

Shriver pulled a bottle and two glasses out of a drawer and set them on the desk. 'Thought you'd want this.'

A shiver ran through Coe as he stared at the bottle. That stuff had put him through the worst hours of his life. He wouldn't vow he'd never touch a drop again, but right now, it was the furthest thing from his mind.

'I don't want a damned drink,' he said violently.

That could be relief in Shriver's sigh. 'You don't know how glad I am to hear you say that, Coe.' He put the glasses and bottle back into the drawer. 'I think we can go ahead and talk now.'

Coe glared at him. Now he knew it was coming. Well, he didn't have to sit here a second longer than he wanted to.

'Did you know Myra had a loan with the bank that's almost due?' Shriver asked.

Coe blinked. That was something he didn't know, but he couldn't see what he could do about it.

Shriver made a tent of his fingers and peered over them. 'I turned Kincaid down on an extension. I considered him a bad risk.'

Coe's thoughts were spinning. Why was Shriver telling him all this?

'The bank doesn't want the stage line,' Shriver went on. 'But it does want its money.'

'You came to the wrong man,' Coe said heatedly. 'I didn't have anything to do with the stage line.'

'You could have,' Shriver said gently. 'The community needs the stage line's services. All those employees need their jobs. I think Myra would be happy to know that you're taking over.'

Coe shook his head in bewilderment. 'You're out of your mind,' he said harshly. 'I haven't got a dime.' What Shriver just said was the most ridiculous thing Coe ever heard. He searched his mind for arguments to bolster his stand. 'What the hell do I know about running a stage line?'

Shriver reprovingly shook his head. 'You should know about it. You grew up around the Bannock Company. You've seen Myra run it. You saw the things she did to make it a success. You can't be that thickheaded not to have learned something.'

Coe blew out a violent breath. Shriver was steadily hemming him in, and it was making him frantic. 'All right,' he admitted. 'I know something about horses. I can keep a stage in repair. I can keep a schedule, but what the hell else do I know? I'd be lost in that office. Just looking at all that paperwork makes my head ache. Damn it, the paperwork is what keeps the line going.' He couldn't believe it, but that was genuine amusement in Shriver's smile.

'You've got Westhoff, haven't you?' Shriver raised a hand, stopping Coe's protest. 'I know Kincaid fired him. But if you were running things, you could give him his job back, couldn't you? All the old personnel are still there, aren't they? I know how much Brad and Myra thought of you. Myra would be pleased to think the business was going on.'

Shriver pointed an accusing finger at Coe. 'I know you'd be the one she would pick.' His voice softened. 'Are you going to let her down?'

Coe's mouth was a thin line in a pale face. 'I wouldn't even know where to start.'

Shriver sadly shook his head. 'I never thought you were one to run from a job that needs doing. The bank will give you all the help it can. You could try it for six months, couldn't you? By then, we'll be able to see how it's going.'

Coe was numb with shock. He had never dared dream this big. He wanted to yell his refusal, and something in him wouldn't let him say the words. He could give it a try, couldn't he? Didn't he owe that much to Brad and Myra?

He drew a deep breath to steady himself, and his grin was shaky. 'I could give it a try,' he said. He was surprised to hear how firm his voice was.

Shriver stood, a beaming smile on his face. He whacked Coe on the shoulder. 'Good, good.'

Coe stood and walked with Shriver to the door. All his depression was gone. 'I'll be back here often, asking for your advice,' he threatened.

'The door's open, Coe.'

Coe stepped outside. He was ten feet tall, and his feet didn't touch the ground.

He wasn't surprised to find Kirby waiting for him. After this day, nothing would surprise him.

'Jude, do you know what he did?' Coe burst forth. 'He wants me to run the stage line.'

'We talked it over earlier this morning,' Kirby said. 'He asked me what I thought, and I told him you could be his man.'

He cocked an eye at Coe. 'You don't look too happy about it.'

'I've got so damned many things to do,' Coe said. 'I've got to find Westhoff and Cummings and get them to come back to work. Then I've got to learn how to run a stage line.'

Kirby shook his head. 'I expected to find you walking on air, and here you look like you see a ghost.'

'I guess I do,' Coe confessed. 'Jude, I'm scared.'

'You should be,' Kirby retorted. 'I'd be disappointed in you if you weren't scared. This is the biggest thing you've ever taken hold of. I'd knock your ears down if you were cocky about it.'

Coe allowed himself a brief, happy laugh.

'I was just wondering if Bill knows about all this. He used to look at me and shake his head. I wonder if he knows all his work on me wasn't wasted?'

'Coe,' Kirby said softly, 'I wouldn't be at all surprised that he knows.'

This Large Print Book, for people
who cannot read normal print,
is published under the auspices of

THE ULVERSCROFT FOUNDATION

NE

VIOLET